**Sayi**

My other books:
*Shelter from Thunder*
*Slaughter in Barnaby Close*
*Shades of Grey*
*Underneath*
*Bits of Cargill*
*Jake*


Email - mcargill79@gmail.com
Twitter - @MichaelCargill1
http://www.facebook.com/MichaelCargillAuthor
Website of hilarity - http://michaelcargill.wordpress.com


*Many thanks are owed to the group moderators on
Goodreads and to those who helped with the editing:*
OCD Reader
Patti
Ignite
Elle
Lindsay
Joo
Tonya
Amy Hildebrand
Everyone else on the UK Amazon Kindle group on
Goodreads

# Chapter 1

*In 1933, Hitler and the National Socialist party rose to power in Germany. A dark cloud of anti-Semitism followed in their wake.*

*In 1939, the German army invaded Poland. A mere five weeks later, Poland surrendered.*

*In 1940, the Nazis created a ghetto in Warsaw, the Polish capital. Nearly half a million Jews were herded into an area designed to hold only a few thousand.*

When Abigail wiggled her toes, the tops of her shoes rippled as if a small rabbit were burrowing around inside them. In the past the idea that a cute little bunny might be living inside her socks would have made her smile, but these days the world seemed to be utterly devoid of laughter. The shoes had been black in colour when she first started wearing them but now they were scuffed and scratched down to a dull grey. Abigail wondered how long it would be until holes started appearing in them and she worried about the problems that such an eventuality would bring. How can you keep your feet clean when your shoes are worn out? And how are you supposed to afford new shoes when the high price means you might not be able to eat for a few days?

Abigail closed her eyes and thought back to when she first received them. It had been her birthday and she loved birthdays. Her father had handed her an oblong box that was wrapped in a nice sheet of blue paper and it was all sealed up with a pretty pink bow. It was the biggest birthday present she had ever received and her eyes were wide with wonder. She set it down on the floor and pulled carefully at the ribbon - it was such a delightful thing that she wanted to keep hold of it afterwards.

"Oh, hurry up and open it," demanded her impatient brother, although Abigail barely even heard him.

The wrapping paper fell away, exposing a plain brown box with the word *Abigail* stencilled neatly and expertly across the front. After lifting the lid off, a pair of the shiniest shoes she had ever seen stared back at her. She discarded the tissue paper -

which seemed cheap and flimsy compared to everything else - and turned the shoes over in her small hands.

"Now aren't they a sight for sore eyes?" exclaimed her mother.

"They look squeaky clean!" added her father.

Although Abigail didn't quite understand these sayings, she could tell that her parents were pleased for her. She tried the shoes on and walked around the room a few times, making sure to avoid going too near her brother - she didn't want him stepping on them and making them dirty. She wore the shoes for the entire day, proudly showing them off to everyone she saw. When night time finally rolled around, Abigail put them back into the box and slid it under her bed. She even decided to keep the tissue paper, as such a pretty pair of shoes deserved to have a comfy little bed to lie in.

After a while, she decided to keep them for special occasions and for when they visited the local synagogue on Saturdays. With her smart shoes she felt like one of the grownups, and it was always nice when someone commented on how pretty she looked. The good thing about being around the grownups was that they never pushed her over, or called her nasty names.

Sometimes she became bored of being around adults all the time, so she would go off and play with the small children. The good thing about being with the small children was that they never pushed her over, or called her nasty names.

If the day was warm and sunny, she would take them outside and teach them how to make daisy chains. Some of the kids had clumsy hands, so Abigail would set them the task of collecting up daisies for everyone else. It was tricky making sure that the youngest ones knew how to pick them with the stalks still attached, but she knew how important it was that everyone was able to join in with the fun. Sometimes she would make small crowns for them to wear on their heads, whilst on other days they would make longer chains to skip and dance around the gardens with.

On the days when it was cold and raining, Abigail would take them off to one of the side rooms and show them how to make animals by folding up a sheet of paper. She loved the look of wonder on the children's faces as she completed the last few folds, causing a sheep or a horse to suddenly appear in front of them.

The children would often come to her if they had a cut or a graze that needed cleaning or kissing better, and she would stay with them until they cheered back up again.

Some of the kids liked to draw pictures, and occasionally they would draw one of Abigail and present it to her at the end of the day. She always kept these ones in her bedroom, right next to the shoebox under her bed.

Sadly, all those things were now nothing more than a distant memory. Abigail turned around and glanced about her room. At one end was her brother's bed, a dirty messy thing with scraps of cloth for blankets. Abigail did her best to keep her own bed clean and tidy, but it was almost impossible - soap and hot water were hard to come by, so everything always seemed to be soiled.

She slowly looked around the small apartment that was now their home. Two or three blankets lay in a dusty pile in the corner, marking the spot where Mr Karski slept.

Nobody seemed to know what Mr Karski's first name was and it was now several weeks since anyone had last seen him. Abigail had been wary of him right from the very beginning. He was a tall man, and Abigail didn't think it was possible to be friends with someone who was so large and intimidating. His arms looked as if they were long enough to touch any point in the room, and she sometimes had nightmares about Mr Karski reaching out from his corner and dropping her out the window.

She could tell that her mother didn't like Mr Karski very much either. Whenever he tried to make conversation with her, her answers were always short and terse and she did her best to avoid looking him in the eye. Unfortunately, in a small place like this, it was very hard to keep your distance.

Abigail walked over to the only window in the apartment. The street they were in was tucked away from the busier areas, which was why they had so far been relatively lucky - other than when Mr Karski had been thrust upon them, they had had the place to themselves. She knew of other instances where three or four families were being crammed into one small room.

Through the window she watched as bits of rubbish blew down the street. The buildings on the other side of the road had cracks running down the walls, whilst some parts of the brickwork were covered with small holes. When they first moved here Abigail thought they were from someone using a drill or a hammer, but it turned out that they were actually bullet holes.

A bit further off into the distance she could see the remains of a bombed out building. Smoke always seemed to be rising from somewhere amongst the ruins and today was no different. Abigail couldn't tell if was because the building was still on fire or because someone was cooking something.

Her attention was drawn to a man on a bicycle riding down the street. The bike itself had a red frame and white-rimmed tires, whilst the horizontal bar had a strip of cloth tied to it. This wasn't the first time she had seen the man out riding his bike and it cheered her up to see him cycling past. She wondered who he was and where he was going, and whether he had any children the same age as her. As the man disappeared from view, Abigail accidentally banged her head on the glass as she tried to follow him as he disappeared round the corner.

"Abbie? Are you okay?" asked a sleepy voice.

Abigail rubbed at her forehead, feeling mildly embarrassed. "Yes, Mum. Just looking out the window."

"Make sure you don't get seen by any soldiers. You know what they're like."

Yes, Abigail knew what the soldiers were like. She had seen that quite clearly on the very first day that they had been brought here.

An unexpected noise from outside the apartment door startled her. Had the soldiers seen her at the window, or was it -

The door opened and a boy in his late teens walked in. He cast a quick glance at the pile of blankets in the corner, before giving Abigail a quick nod. Abigail smiled tentatively back at him.

"Leo? Is that you?" asked the sleepy voice.

"Yes, Mum. I've got us something to eat, come on out."

There was a squeak of bed springs and a few moments later a tired looking woman appeared in the doorway of a gloomy room. She was wearing a long dress, a jumper, and a tatty cardigan.

"Sorry, I was asleep again," said his mother.

Leo didn't say anything. His mother seemed to be sleeping a lot these days, something that worried him a great deal. He didn't know if it was because of the exhaustion from the lack of food or because she was ill; maybe it was both.

Reaching from under his coat, he pulled out a package and placed it on the bare wooden table in the middle of the apartment. Inside the package was a loaf of bread and a tin can that didn't have a label. Abigail let out an exclamation of surprise and looked over at her mother, who was rubbing her eyes as if she thought she was hallucinating.

"If someone cuts the bread, I'll open the tin," Leo told them.

His mother grabbed them a plate each - their *only* plates - whilst Abigail sat down at the table and waited as the bread was shared out between them. Leo grunted with frustration as he worked the blunt tin opener around the edges of the tin, whilst his mother and sister watched in fascinated silence.

"Finally!" Leo announced, wiping a dirty hand across his forehead.

He carefully prised the lid back, making sure that he didn't prick himself on any of the sharp edges - cuts and grazes always seemed to take longer to heal these days. The sweet smell of fruit filled their nostrils, a pleasant change from the stench of dirt and dust, and Leo used a fork to dish the peach slices out between them. Abigail stared at this curious meal of bread and fruit, wondering which one to start with. She knew that fruit was usually saved for dessert, but what was she supposed to do with the bread?

"Never had a peach sandwich before?" Leo asked good naturedly. He shoved his slices between two bits of bread and took a big bite.

It was one of the most substantial meals they had had for several weeks and the three of them ate hungrily and in silence. Leo worked through his food quickly, stopping only to rescue any pieces of fruit that tried to squirm out the sides of the sandwich. He watched his sister with fascination, a small smile spreading across his face - she always managed to do everything so neatly and daintily, barely spilling so much as a crumb onto her plate.

He glanced over at his mother and was glad to see that she didn't look quite so tired now. She was far thinner than she used to be, but that was true for pretty much everyone here in the ghetto.

5

Finishing his meal before they did, he grabbed the tin and took a sip of the remaining juice. It tasted good and he let out a belch to register his satisfaction. The three of them looked at each other and burst into a fit of giggles. All of sudden a huge weight was lifted from their shoulders, breaking the tension that always seemed to hang over them these days.

Although Abigail and her mother also drank some of the juice, neither of them managed to produce any comical noises afterwards - whether this was because of a lifetime of ingrained table manners, or because they simply didn't know how to force it even if they wanted to, Leo was unable to say.

"Daddy liked peaches," Abigail noted absently.

She went quiet as her mother and brother looked at her. Although there wasn't any anger in their eyes, their stares still managed to make her feel self-conscious.

"Yes, he really did," agreed Leo.

"God bless him," added their mother.

Yes, he had liked peaches a great deal. Their larder back at their old home - their *real* home - always had at least half a dozen tins of them stacked up on the shelves and they used to joke that the local shopkeeper would go out of business if they decided to move away from the area. If their father was ever working in his study, you could almost guarantee that he would be dutifully working his way through a freshly opened tin and he even had a favourite fork that he kept hidden in his desk drawer.

"Remember when we bought those tins just before his birthday?" Leo asked. "We swapped the labels round, and he got the shock of his life when he saw that it was just peas inside them."

Both his sister and his mother laughed at the memory. All three of them had been in on the joke, although Abigail thought that it was a bit of a mean thing to do on someone's birthday. She eventually warmed to the idea, and they gave her the task of making sure that the labels were glued back on straight. When the big day arrived, Abigail had been the one who laughed the loudest once that first tin had been opened.

Abigail was the last to finish her sandwich and she picked at the few crumbs that were left on her plate. "Thanks, Leo," she said in a quiet voice.

Leo nodded at her. Their hunger had been postponed rather than sated, and he didn't know where the next lot of food was going to come from.

"Where did you get it from?" asked his mother. The look on her face suggested that she didn't actually want to know.

Leo shrugged. "I've got some friends who can help us out."

Abigail looked at him with interest. "I'd like some friends. Maybe I could go up to the orphanage and help out with the children."

Their mother raised her eyebrows. "You might even get a hot meal there."

Leo frowned. "It's too dangerous out there for you."

In fact, it was dangerous out there for everyone. Although Leo supposed that his sister probably could get some kind of job at the orphanage, what if she left for work one morning and was never seen again? He'd be devastated.

"It really would help though," Abigail persisted. She looked hurt at having her suggestion rebuffed so quickly and easily.

"Maybe, I don't know. Something might turn up," Leo replied noncommittally.

When Abigail glanced over at the discarded pile of blankets in the corner, a chill ran down her spine. She tried to remember what Mr Karski looked like but couldn't recall anything other than his long arms, his long legs, his long nose, and his long face. In her mind he had somehow changed from being a real person to the sort of fairytale troll who came and stole young children from their beds.

"We may as well make use of those blankets," Leo said. "He won't be needing them as he isn't coming back."

Leo picked up the empty tin can in front him and twirled it around in his hand. In any other world, this empty metal husk had served its purpose and would be discarded along with all the other rubbish. In the world that they now lived in, it was an object with value. It could be used to drink from, it could be used to cook something in, and it could even be used to dig up potatoes. For the truly desperate, it could even be placed on the mantelpiece and admired like a vase or a small clock. In a world where you have nothing, everything has a value of some kind.

When Leo put the can back down on the table, Abigail picked it up and turned it over in her hands. The edges were sharp and dangerous, making it look like the mouth of a giant flesh eating worm. She slowly twisted the lid off, folded it neatly down the middle and swirled it around in front of her.

"It's like a shiny little butterfly," she announced.

There was a moment of silence, causing Abigail to suddenly feel self-conscious again. Just as she began to withdraw back into her shell, her mother burst out laughing and clasped her hands together. Leo smiled and shook his head at her.

Leo pushed the can in her direction. "Can you make me a mansion, please?" he teased, sending his mother into another bout of laughter.

Abigail looked warily at her brother. Although his smile seemed genuine, she couldn't shake the feeling that he was mocking her. She glanced over at her mother and saw that she too was smiling. It was a happy, joyous smile that Abigail hadn't seen for a long time and the tiredness had been banished from her face. When she looked back at Leo, Abigail realised he was only playing and she let out a small giggle.

"My dear girl, you're such a sweet little thing. That's cheered me right up," her mother told her.

Although it pleased Abigail to hear her mother say that, she was a little embarrassed too: it hadn't been her intention to make them laugh as if she was some kind of clown. If she was honest, Abigail wasn't really sure what kind of reaction she had been expecting - she had slipped off into her own little dream world and the spark of an idea had popped into her head. Even as she was prising off the lid she didn't really know what she was going to do with it, but bending the thin metal seemed like an obvious thing to do and her imagination had done the rest.

As the evening wore on the room slowly descended into darkness and the three of them remained at the table until it was almost impossible to see each other. Although they had the option of lighting some candles, there didn't seem to be much point in wasting them for tonight. Leo could feel his own hunger returning and he was pretty sure the other two could as well. He had initially planned to save some of the food for tomorrow, but the moment he walked through the door and caught sight of the hopeful – not to mention desperate – looks on their faces, he knew that there was no way he was going to be able to stick with that plan. Chances are that they would regret it in the coming days, but the boost in morale – no matter how short-lived it might be – was worth it.

Abigail decided to keep hold of the empty can. She didn't know what she was going to do with it, but it seemed a pity to let good things go to waste. Perhaps if she flattened it out with a stone she could do something with it, or maybe if she found another can she could attach some string to them and use them as stilts.

Their mother yawned. "Well, it's nearly pitch black in here and I'm starting to feel tired again," she told them. "Thanks for the food, Leo. And thanks for the laugh, Abbie."

Leo picked up the blankets from the corner of the room and handed one to his mother as she went off to her room again. There was a squeak of springs as she climbed back into bed.

"Some of your clothes are getting holes in them again, Leo. I'll see if I can repair them tomorrow, I should be feeling better then," she called out to him.

As far Leo as was concerned his clothes were fine, but he knew how much his mother still liked to mother him.

Abigail slipped into the room that she shared with her brother and carefully placed the can under her bed, wary that he might tease her again if he realised what she was doing. The air had turned chilly and a shiver ran through her as she stepped out of her shoes and placed her feet onto the bare wooden floor. Even though she now had an extra blanket, it was likely to be a rough night of tossing and turning before she got to sleep.

Leo came into the room and sat on his bed. He pulled his shoes off, letting them drop loudly onto the floor. Abigail slid her own shoes delicately under the bed.

"Night, Abbie," he said.

"Night," she replied. "It's going to be cold tonight."

Leo propped himself up on one elbow. "You can come and sleep in here if you want to keep warm," he told her.

Abigail hesitated for a moment, wondering if this was the lead-in to a mean boys trick. She tip-toed silently across the dark

9

room, startling Leo when her black shape suddenly appeared in front of him. She lifted the covers and slid in next to him.

"Thanks, Leo," she whispered.

Leo turned over onto his side and put a protective arm around his sister; lying next to him like this, she seemed so small and fragile.

He closed his eyes, let out a sigh and allowed himself to drift off to sleep.

***

# Chapter 2

The next morning, Leo was the first one to wake up. It was cosy and warm in the bed so he was content to just lie there for a while, slipping in and out of a light doze. Abigail stirred and let out a small cough but quickly settled back down again.

Leo was unable to ignore the pressure on his bladder any longer and eased himself carefully off the bed. After using the toilet he decided against flushing it - the water supply was erratic at best, so they used it sparingly. He tried the tap in the sink and was relieved when a weak trickle wormed out. He filled his hands with water and splashed it over his face, before brushing some through his hair. The small cracked mirror over the sink revealed a grubby face that hadn't seen a bar of soap for a while. After washing as best as he could, Leo walked over to what was the kitchen area. The cupboards were as bare as he had expected them to be, which made the hunger pangs all the more unbearable.

Leo went back into the bedroom and saw that Abigail was now awake. She looked up at him and sleepily murmured something.

"There's a little bit of water in the taps at the moment," he told her, jerking his thumb behind him.

She sat up and yawned, rubbing at her eyes. After quickly scooting past her brother, she bent down and retrieved her shoes out from under her bed.

"Are they your birthday shoes?" he asked her. There was a hint of dismay in his voice.

She smiled at him and nodded, before disappearing off to the bathroom.

Leo sat down at the table in the middle of the apartment. There was a squeak of bed springs and a few seconds later his mother appeared in the doorway of her bedroom. Although she still wore the appearance of someone who had just woken up, Leo was glad to see that the look of outright exhaustion had disappeared.

She coughed a couple of times. "We're going to need to go to the market or something today, there's nothing in the cupboards," she told him.

11

"I know, I looked earlier. Abbie's in the bathroom at the moment," Leo replied, changing the subject.

She nodded. A trip to the market was one thing; actually having the means to pay was another issue entirely.

His mother sat down at the table and waited for the bathroom to become free. When Abigail came out, she smiled at her mother and walked over to the window. A lone man shuffled slowly along the street below her. It looked as if he was wearing sandals, which seemed odd considering how cold it could be out there. When she looked again, Abigail realised that they weren't sandals at all - they were just normal shoes that were falling apart.

Out the corner of her eye, she saw something creeping towards the window. Her eyes darted to the right and fell upon a spider crawling its way along the wall. Abigail let out a small sound of joy and carefully scooped the little creature up into her hand. She let it run over her fingers, giggling as she felt the tickling sensation of its tiny legs against her skin.

Behind her, Leo grimaced. He didn't like spiders or anything else that crawled or buzzed or wormed its way through life. Swatting an insect with a rolled up newspaper was about as intimate as he was willing to get, and he had no idea how his sister could stomach playing with them like that. For the next minute he watched as she allowed the spider to run up and down her arms, gracefully twirling her hands around so she could control where it went. An expression of childlike wonder settled on her face, one that usually meant she was once again slipping into her own little dream world.

Abigail slowly turned round to face her brother, her hands dancing and swirling through the air. For a fleeting moment she looked like a ballerina, and Leo found himself captivated by the sight of her.

She smiled across the room at him. "An incy wincy spider," she remarked.

Leo smiled back at her, momentarily joining her in the dream world she so often retreated into. It was a warm and pleasant place that he didn't want to be removed from.

The sound of the toilet being flushed jerked both of them back to reality. Abigail's spider fell to the floor and scurried off to a corner somewhere. Their mother walked noisily out from the bathroom.

"We off out then?" she asked. If she hadn't been adjusting her clothes she would have seen the annoyed looks on their faces.

Leo nodded wearily and stood up, whilst Abigail let out a small sigh.

Their apartment was at the top of a set of cold concrete steps and they trudged their way down them. Near the bottom step was a small round hole in the wall that Abigail claimed had been made by a mouse, although Leo thought it was more likely to be a bullet hole. Another door lay just beyond the foot of the stairs, whilst the outside world awaited them on the other side. Or at least, the portion of the outside world that they were allowed into.

The three of them stepped out onto the street and walked towards the main ghetto square. Every so often the smell of human excrement and urine wafted around them. Abigail caught sight of a discarded pile of rags down a narrow alleyway but it wasn't until they moved that she realised it was a person lying on the ground.

They walked past a large bombed-out building. It wasn't much more than a large mound of broken red bricks and protruding wooden beams, but Abigail often saw children using it as a playground. A lone doorway stood resolute and defiant at the front of the rubble.

The closer they got to where the market stalls were, the busier the roads became. Numerous other families shuffled along nervously in tight groups, seeking protection in numbers. They came across a bearded old man standing on a street corner, shifting his weight from one foot to the other. He repeatedly turned his head one way and then another, almost as if he were watching a tennis match that only he could see. When he caught sight of Abigail's wide-eyed stares, he waved eagerly at her; she didn't wave back.

German soldiers were dotted around the place, some of them standing in groups whilst others stood alone. They seemed little more than disturbing creatures of harsh black boots and intimidating uniforms.

Abigail caught sight of something moving on the roof of a small building, sending a surge of childish delight running through her.

"Look up there!" she cried. "A cat!"

Although several people looked up in the direction she was pointing, no-one said anything. Leo gritted his teeth in frustration.

Abigail was still looking up at the sleek black feline when a frown appeared on her face.

"I wonder who looks after it," she wondered aloud. "Who feeds it?"

Leo glared down at her. Out here on the street he despised her innocence - it was the sort of thing that could get her killed. He had a good idea about how a natural predator like a cat would keep itself alive in a place like this... assuming, of course, that no-one else tried to catch it and cook it first.

"No-one living, that's for sure," he growled at her.

Abigail looked at him in confusion for a few moments. As his words sank in, she felt herself shrinking back into her shell.

"Oh, come on it's nothing like that," her mother reassured her. "They're scavengers, they only eat scraps." She frowned at her son, who just shrugged and looked away.

They walked past a man who had a bizarre array of items laid out on a blanket in front of him. There was a belt that didn't have a buckle; some old and twisted bits of stiff brown leather; what looked to be a soiled bandage; a crumpled, empty box of matches; and a pile of sticks.

Abigail stopped and looked at them with mild interest.

"You want one, little girl? I'll do you a good price," the man said to her. There was an unsettling desperation in his voice, as if he had been trying to sell these things for weeks.

Abigail opened her mouth to say something and then closed it again. The man's eyes were red and full of despair, whilst his hunched back made it look as if he was going to fall on top of her. Just as he began to move in her direction, she ran off and caught up with Leo and her mother.

As she rejoined them, Leo glanced down at his sister. Abigail was worried that he was going to snap at her again, but instead he placed a comforting hand on the small of her back. They soon came to a table that was covered in vegetables. Carrots, cauliflowers, and potatoes were arranged in bulging piles right in front of them.

To Abigail's eyes the cauliflowers looked so fresh and white they could be mistaken for snowballs. The carrots were so bright and juicy that they could be used as a torch in the darkness, whilst the potatoes looked heavy enough to break any plate you might try to eat one on. Standing behind the table was a middle aged woman. She was wearing odd, unmatching clothes and old bits of blankets, making it hard to see where one garment ended and another one began.

"How much are the carrots?" Abigail wondered out loud.

The woman looked at her for a few moments, causing Abigail to regret saying anything - her brother was better at dealing with this sort of thing than she was.

"Depends what you got to give," the woman told her.

Leo cleared his throat and quoted the price that he remembered from the week before.

The woman grunted. "Not likely. Price is about double that now, give or take a bit."

"That's outrageous!" their mother said, her face turning red. "How do you expect anyone to afford that?"

The woman shrugged. "Don't blame me. You know what it's like when we get a load of new arrivals in here, all flush with money and buying up the food for themselves. And then when it runs out in a few days' time, they'll be selling their furniture to pay for more. And then when their supplies run down again, they'll be selling their clothes." The woman paused to catch her breath. "God only knows what they do after that."

Abigail and her mother stood there in a dumbstruck silence, whilst Leo clenched his fists and gritted his teeth in frustration. The woman looked at him warily and took a small step back.

"Well, maybe we can sort something out," she suggested. "You got a watch or some jewellery?"

The thought of having to barter for food made Leo angry. He remembered when his family had initially been herded into this place: they had been one of the aforementioned new arrivals, all flush with money and buying up all the available food.

The way in which the food was distributed disgusted him - why should it only be the wealthy who got to eat? The Germans

15

purposefully undersupplied them, and this free market nonsense meant they were all playing right into the Nazis' hands. By creating the haves and the have-nots, they were forcing a wedge between themselves. It was divide and conquer at its worst.

"What about your belt? I can probably do you something if it's a good one," the woman told him. She spoke as if she was doing him some kind of favour.

Unfortunately, Leo's 'belt' was nothing more than a length of string. He looked down at the carrots and fought back the urge to grab one and use it as a club to beat her with. A man came and stood next to them. After a brief discussion with the woman, he thrust some money into her hand and disappeared with a bundle tucked under his coat. Leo glared after him.

"Come on, let's go somewhere else," he told his sister and mother.

He stormed off and they had to walk quickly to catch him up.

"What are we going to do?" his mother asked.

He remained quiet for a few moments. "Just follow me; I know where we can get some help."

They walked near a lone German soldier. In his hand was a cigarette lighter and he absently flicked at the flint with his thumb. Abigail stared at him, thinking that the little spark was like watching a tiny fairy being forced to dance for her cruel taskmaster. The soldier glared sullenly back at her and grunted with displeasure.

Leo led them for another couple of minutes and stopped beside a non-descript building. He bent down and undid his shoe, tipping it upside down as if he were trying to get rid of a troublesome stone. As he put it back on, he glanced quickly around him to make sure that there were no soldiers nearby.

"This way," he said quietly.

Leo turned down the side of the building and knocked briskly on the first door they came to. A few seconds later the door opened a crack and a corner of a scruffy face peered out at them.

"We need some help," Leo said. "Can we come in?"

Abigail's heart sank as the face disappeared and the door clicked shut. Further up along the alley she spotted a black shape moving around. Although she hoped that it was the cat she had seen earlier, it was more likely to be a rat. From behind the door came an odd metallic rattling sound and Abigail briefly wondered if someone was pulling a huge chain that was going to open a hidden trapdoor from under their feet.

The door opened again and a man with a scruffy face gestured for them to hurry inside. Abigail was the last one in, and she had to dodge out of the way as the man began closing the door before she was inside.

The floor was bare and dusty, making their shoes sound loud and heavy on the wooden floorboards. Abigail once again heard the metallic rattling sound from behind her but she resisted the temptation to turn around and look. They went down some stairs and through another door. Abigail wrinkled her nose as the faint smell of steam, warmth, and cooking drifted towards her. They went through a doorway and entered a wide room that was populated with two-dozen people of all ages. There was a short queue over to one side and the three of them patiently joined the back of it. A pile of dented white metallic bowls was stacked up on a table and Leo grabbed one for each of them. Abigail spotted an ant crawling across her own bowl and she tilted it around as she watched it trying to escape. A woman used a ladle with a long handle to scoop two lots of soup into her bowl, whilst another woman at the end of the table handed her a slice of bread. A knob of butter was clinging to the end of it, and Abigail thought that it looked like a small piece of sunshine.

The room was filled with tables of varying heights and sizes, with people sitting on boxes, stools, and chairs. Over in one corner was a rabbi talking to a small group of people, and Leo purposefully chose a seat that was facing away from him.

"How long has this place been here?" his mother asked.

"Not that long," Leo told her. "The Germans recently discovered one of the other soup kitchens and smashed the place up."

Abigail used her finger to spread the butter over the bread. She battled briefly with indecision, before shoving the finger into her mouth to lick the remainder off.

Leo watched her with a small smile on his face. He couldn't imagine her doing that in their old life; instead, she would have used a napkin to wipe her hand clean.

Abigail realised with dismay that she had forgotten to pick up a spoon. Leo handed her his own spoon and grabbed a discarded one that was lying on another table. She smiled at him and began to eat.

Leo finished his meal first and leaned back in his chair. The room they were all sitting in looked as if it had once served as a basement storage area. The lights hanging down from the ceiling were erratically placed, which suggested that they were a recent addition. He found it interesting that the people running this operation were able to secure a reliable supply of gas and electricity. It was impossible for him to say for sure, but he had an idea of how it had been done: the German policy of indiscriminately herding Polish Jews into the ghetto meant that people of all professions ended up here. In an odd twist of fate the shopkeepers, solicitors, and accountants of the outside world suddenly found themselves utterly redundant. It was the electricians, plumbers, and engineers who were now amongst the most coveted people - their skills were needed in order to secure water and power for places like this. By tapping into the existing infrastructure just about anything was possible... provided you could pay for it.

The same was true for some of the darker professions, too: several pick pockets, smugglers, and thieves were surprised to discover that they were now welcomed by society rather than shunned. More than one German officer had discovered that his wallet was suddenly lighter than it had been earlier in the day.

Leo turned around and saw that the rabbi was still sitting in the corner and talking to a group of people. The rabbi made a gesture with his hands, and Leo felt a rush of anger when he saw that his fingers and wrists were weighed down with gold jewellery. As far as he was concerned, such flagrant displays of wealth were outrageous in a place like this. He thought back to the woman in the marketplace who had wanted an incredible sum of money in exchange for a few vegetables - how was it fair that this rabbi was wielding so much wealth when there were people out there going hungry? Those rings and trinkets could be sold and the resulting funds used to buy food.

The rabbi seemed to feel his glare and he nodded and waved a hand at Leo. Leo was caught off guard and nodded back involuntarily. He turned back around and saw that his mother and sister were almost finished. The spoon that he had given to Abigail was too big for her mouth, and Leo smiled to himself as he watched her struggle with it.

"You can go up for another helping once you're finished," he told them. "Not straight away, though. There's only so much to go around."

They glanced up and nodded gratefully at him.

Once Abigail had finished she laid her spoon down in the bowl as her mother had always told her to. Good table manners cost nothing and you never know who might be watching. Just over her brother's shoulder she caught sight of the rabbi sitting in the corner. His presence was familiar and comforting, even if the cramped surroundings weren't.

Although she didn't really understand the things that the rabbi at their local synagogue talked about, he had always been kind and polite to her and was also a regular visitor to their house. Sometimes he would come round for dinner, which meant that they would get to use the good china that was only ever brought out for special occasions. Abigail liked it when they had guests round for meals and she would help her mother set the table during the day. The dishes had matching flower patterns on them, whilst the cutlery was so shiny that it seemed to sparkle like rows of diamonds - everything looked so pretty that it was almost a shame to put food on it.

Other times when the rabbi came round, it would only be for tea and cake in the afternoon. He shared their father's fondness for peaches and it wouldn't be long before a couple of tins were cracked open. There was no eating out of the tins when the rabbi was round though - the fruit would always be served up in proper bowls, smothered with fresh cream, and eaten with a spoon. Sometimes they would take it up into her father's study and eat whilst they chatted about adult things. Abigail was always fascinated with what they talked about in her father's office. She had tried listening in at the door a few times, but all she could ever

19

hear was the muffled sound of their voices and the occasional outburst of laughter.

Once the rabbi went home again, her father would often forget to bring the dirty bowls back down with him. They would remain up there until their mother found them, the insides all clogged up with green mould. It made her furious and she would shout at him for being such a stupid man.

Leo kept an eye on the queue for the food, patiently waiting until there were a few more people in the line. Somewhere in the back of his mind a nagging voice was telling him that going up for a second helping was abusing the system: there were plenty of people who hadn't had anything at all yet.

"Come on, let's go up again," he said in a low voice.

The three of them rejoined the queue and got themselves another helping. One of the serving women gave Leo a quick wink and he grinned bashfully back at her. Abigail spotted a spoon that was smaller than the one she had been using so she grabbed it before anyone else could. They sat back down in the same seats as before and resumed their meal. They ate slower this time, knowing that they would have to leave afterwards. Before they finished, the rabbi got up and left. Leo watched him go without interest, whilst Abigail wanted to know if he liked peaches.

Leo looked around the room again and wondered if this place would still be here in six months' time. What if the tables and the chairs were needed by people desperate for warmth and something to cook food on? What if it was discovered by the Germans? The soldiers would come down here with their truncheons and fists to smash the place up, beating women, children, and old men alike until they lay unconscious. If the soldiers were drunk they would wave their pistols around, firing shots into the floor or the ceiling to scare people, whilst the more sporting types wouldn't have any qualms about putting a bullet or two into some unfortunate soul's head.

The three of them finished their second helpings and remained in their seats for a while longer. Abigail traced her finger around the inside of her bowl, licking up the small scraps that were left over. Leo watched her do it, noting that most other kids her age would simply use their tongue to clean the bowl.

"They should put some paintings up in here, it'd make the place look nicer," she remarked, mostly to herself.

Although Leo found it hard to disagree with his sister on this point, he was sceptical about how many artists would actually feel like picking up their paintbrushes.

"We should probably get going," he told them. "I don't like staying in these places for too long, it gets..." Leo shrugged and let the sentence trail off. He wasn't sure how to describe what he meant. The stench of desperation was strong everywhere you went, but there was something unsettling about watching so many people wolf down a bowl of watery soup as if it might be their last ever meal.

On one of the tables, Abigail spotted a discarded slice of bread. She glanced around but couldn't see who it might belong to, and was filled with an overwhelming urge to take it for herself. She had never stolen anything before in her life, but it seemed a pity to let good food go to waste. What if the place was closed when they came back next time? Her belly would be demanding to know why she passed up the opportunity to consume a few extra precious calories.

She grabbed it and started folding it neatly in half to put into her pocket for later. A heavy hand suddenly clamped down on her shoulder, sending a flash of panic rushing through her mind. Was she going to be thrown out and told to never come back? Had her foolish greed branded all three of them as being untrustworthy thieves? Abigail noticed that the hand was grubby and the fingernails were filled with dirt. She dared a glance behind her, her eyes widening in panic and desperation until she was peering up at a familiar face.

Leo looked down at his sister's panic-ridden expression and winked at her. "That's my girl," he whispered.

A mixture of relief, embarrassment, and guilt swam around in her head. She tucked the bread into her coat pocket and just about managed to give Leo a weak smile.

As the three of them walked towards the exit, Abigail noticed a blonde girl wearing a red cap sitting at one of the tables. She seemed to be staring at something - or someone - very intently, and there was a tiny, barely perceptible nod of her head. Abigail followed the girl's gaze and found herself looking at her brother again. Although she couldn't be certain, Abigail was sure that Leo had been looking at the blonde girl.

Abigail wondered who this mysterious female was and why she might have been looking at her brother like that. Was it one of his friends that he often spoke about? The more she thought about it, the more Abigail realised that she didn't know anything about Leo's so-called friends - he never actually spoke about them, merely mentioned them in passing every now and then.

As they made their way back up the stairs, Abigail could feel the warmth and the comforting smell of food slowly fading away. When they reached the front door, the same scruffy man was standing guard. Leo thanked him, and that strange rattling sound of a chain being dragged across something large made Abigail feel on edge. She was the last one out and once again had to skip deftly through the rapidly closing gap to avoid being trapped inside.

"We'll go a slightly different way back home," Leo said. "Can never be too careful."

During the walk back to their apartment, they came upon a partially collapsed wall. Two boys had climbed up the lower side and were walking carefully along the top, their arms outstretched for balance. Abigail was reminded of a tightrope walker she once saw when the circus came to their town. Back then she had been amazed at how someone could climb to such a dizzying height, before effortlessly making his way across a flimsy length of rope.

The two boys were laughing and egging each other on and Abigail watched them with interest. They were nearly at the end of the wall when she suddenly became aware of two German soldiers who were also watching the boys. Although the soldiers were laughing, there was an unpleasantness to their grins that made Abigail feel uneasy. One of them pointed two fingers in the direction of the boys and made a noise like a gun, much to the amusement of the other soldier.

A feeling of dread began to well up inside Abigail and the world seemed to slow down. It was almost as if she were the only one aware of what was going on and she felt utterly powerless to stop it. She wanted to shout at the two boys, to yell at them to get down off that stupid wall because the soldiers were going to hurt them... but she was afraid: afraid of what the boys might do to her if they fell and hurt themselves, afraid of what the soldiers might do if she ruined their fun.

The boys were now only a few feet away from the end of the wall. All it would take was another few steps and they could jump down and be safe.

When she looked back at the soldiers, she saw that one of them had now unshouldered his rifle. The other one made a face that suggested he was trying to work out the odds of his friend being on target.

Abigail's face twitched with fear. Why were these men doing this? Didn't they realise that those boys were only playing? That all they needed to do was to shout something at them? She thought back to when the boys at her school were being naughty. All it required was a stern word from the teacher and they would behave themselves again.

Glancing back at the two boys, Abigail was dismayed when she saw that they were still on the wall. Their steps seemed to be getting smaller, their slow movements getting slower, and in her head she was screaming at them to hurry up.

She looked back at the soldier and let out a whimper when she saw that he was aiming his rifle at the two children. The other one was leaning in towards his friend, looking down the sight as if to make sure that the aim was true. This second soldier muttered something, causing the other one to briefly lower his weapon as he laughed his head off.

Abigail looked back at the wall and was utterly gobsmacked to see that they were *still* up there. Her eyes began flitting back and forth between the boys and the soldiers. With every passing moment the boys seemed to get slower and slower, whilst the soldiers moved faster and faster. The boys would take a tiny step, and the gun would be raised another few inches. The boys would pause to regain their balance, and the soldier would be aiming right down the sight. The boys would take yet *another* tiny step, and the wall seemed to sprout an extra brick and become even longer.

She wanted to go up to the soldiers and shake them, to tell them that the boys are just playing, that if they just asked them nicely they would get down off their wall, and that maybe someone should put a sign up telling them not to play there. She wanted to scream and scream and scream, but her mind was filled with the images of the terrible things they might do to her if she did.

*Just jump. You're at the end of the wall, so just jump! Jump before they get you, jump before they -*

The crack of a rifle boomed and rolled out across the entire world. Tears filled Abigail's eyes as she caught a quick glimpse of the two boys tumbling towards the ground. She covered her face with her hands and began sobbing. Almost immediately she felt someone pulling at her, someone strong who was going to hurt her for making so much noise; hurt her for trying to spoil their fun; hurt her for not shouting out a warning.

"Ssssh, it's okay Abbie," whispered a familiar voice. "The boys are fine, they jumped down just in time."

She looked up into a grubby face, not quite able to believe what the voice was saying. Was this just another nasty boy's trick again? She wiped her eyes and peered round just in time to see two kids running off round the corner. After letting out a halting laugh of relief, she leaned her head against her big powerful brother.

"Did they really jump? Was that really them?" she asked him.

"Yes, it was. And they certainly won't be climbing on that wall again," he told her. He tried to sound soothing, but there was anger and fear in his voice.

Abigail let out a sigh and wiped at her face again. "Sorry, I thought... I thought the soldiers had killed them," she croaked.

"That's okay. I think most people thought the same as you did. Come on, let's go this way."

Leo led them back the way they had come and away from the soldiers. Although he might claim that his motive for doing this was so that his sister wouldn't have to look at them again, he was rather shaken up about it himself. If they were willing to fire at two bored kids walking along the top of a wall, they certainly wouldn't have any qualms about firing at anyone else.

After a couple of minutes, Abigail's tears stopped. She began to feel embarrassed about her emotional outburst and was grateful when her mother put a reassuring arm around her. Once they arrived back at their apartment, Abigail glanced down at the hole as she usually did, looking for any evidence that a mouse really did live there. As ever, there was nothing to see other than dust and the cold - it was as if they were living in some kind of dead zone where even the smallest and most vulnerable things were left to rot and die.

Their mother sat down on one of the chairs and rested her elbows on the table. She rubbed her eyes with her fingers and took a deep breath.

"I think I'm going to volunteer to help out at that soup kitchen place," she announced. "Spending all this time sleeping saps my energy. I feel so useless."

Leo looked at her with a mixture of surprise and relief. He could see that some colour had returned to her cheeks and she didn't look as exhausted as she had done for the past few months.

"That's good," he told her. "You'll be in the warm and you'll be able to eat something other than stale bread."

"I'll probably go tomorrow. I can just about remember the way."

"You're looking better today, Mum. I hope you stay better," Abigail told her.

"Thanks, Abbie. I feel better, really I do."

After a while Leo announced that he was going out again as he had some things to do and would hopefully be able to bring something in for dinner. His mother and sister listened to the sound of his footsteps as he went down the stairs and out the front door. They both felt vulnerable and exposed, almost as if a sign had been put up outside that said *Lone mother and child in here!*

Abigail sat down and started tracing her finger around the table. In her head she was clearing new pathways out of the ghetto, and everyone was joyous and happy as they all escaped back to their old lives again. The soldiers were being arrested and put into prison, forced to stay there until they apologised for all the nasty things they had done.

Chana sat there looking at her daughter. There was a small, pleasant smile on Abigail's face that Chana had seen many times before, one that usually made an appearance when she retreated back into her own little dream world. Her finger moved across the tabletop in swift delicate sweeps, alternating between smooth arcs and sharp right-angles.

Chana remained silent and motionless as Abigail began humming to herself. An odd sensation began to creep through her as she tried to remember the last time she had noticed her daughter going off into her own little world like this.

Abigail suddenly looked up at her mother. Although her humming stopped almost immediately, the dreamy expression on her face lingered for several more moments.

A surge of guilt ran through Chana as she began to think about what she had been doing for the past few months. After her husband died she had been consumed with grief and mourning, shutting out everything else around her. Mr Karski had been thrust into their lives shortly afterwards, which only served to make things worse. Having to put up with such a strange, tall man living in the same apartment as them made her feel ill and she spent most of her time trying to avoid him. Sleeping all day in bed had been the best way to achieve that, and that is precisely what she had ended up doing. If it hadn't been for Leo going out and scrounging for food, they would have starved to death. She realised that she had been neglecting her own children.

Chana reached out and grabbed hold of one of Abigail's small hands. "Abbie," she began, unsure of what to actually say. "Everything's going to work out fine for us. Things will get better, they always do. We Nussbaums have always been smarter than the rest."

Abigail smiled. "I hope so, Mum."

Her mother glanced around the place, noticing how dirty and dusty it was. She stood up and started looking around for some cleaning implements. In the cupboards she managed to find a small dented bucket, a worn out brush, and several rags. There was no soap and the water pressure was low, but that was a problem they could easily work around and for the next couple of hours mother and daughter did their best to get the apartment looking as nice as possible. Abigail was glad to see her mother doing something other than lying in bed all day, whilst Chana was glad to have something constructive to do for once. Once the cleaning was over and done with, Chana went back to her room for a lie down. Although she was feeling better than she had for a long time, she still hadn't recovered all of her strength.

Abigail stood by the window for a while, staring out at the small part of the world she now lived in. She looked towards the bombed out building in the distance, noting that there was no smoke rising up from it at the moment. As her mind began to wander, she tried to imagine what had destroyed it in the first place. Was it a bomb dropped by the Nazis from one of their monstrous planes or was it the work of a shell fired by a tank? What had the building been used for and what happened to all the people inside it? Had they been working or merely seeking shelter from the terrible war that was raging all around them?

She was snapped out of her daze when she spotted the man on the bike rolling down the street again. A frown appeared on her face as the usual questions arose in her mind: who was he and where was he going? Why was he here? In fact, why were any of them here? Why did all the men decide to have a war in the first place? Why had the Germans forced them to leave their home? Why did so many people want to hurt her just because she was Jewish? What did it even mean to be Jewish?

Abigail understood what it was to be a girl and she also understood why the boys and girls at school had separate changing rooms. To a certain degree, she even understood what it was to be Polish. Her teacher had once shown the class a map of their town, one that marked out all the roads, the shops, and the houses. The teacher produced a second map, one which covered the whole of Poland and the class was able to see their town in relation to all the nearby towns and the big bustling cities that they had heard about. Soon afterwards the teacher had produced a third map, this time one that showed the whole of Europe. Abigail found it fascinating to finally see the shapes of all the other important countries that she knew about - Britain, France, Austria, Norway, and Germany. In her head she had always tried to conjure up an image of what those countries would look like based on their name, something that she had often tried to do with people, and it was always a disappointment to discover that someone called Ludwick didn't actually *look* like a Ludwick.

The maps had shown her that Polish people live in Poland, the French people live in the bit called France, whilst the British were all squashed together on an island called Great Britain, all of which made perfect sense to her.

However, she found her Jewishness rather puzzling. As far as she could see, there was very little to differentiate the Jews from the non-Jews - they all used the same changing rooms in school, went to the same shops, and lived in the same streets and towns. They even lived in the same bit of land marked *Poland* on the map. So why did people pick on her for being Jewish?

She remembered one particular day at school, many years ago. It had been a warm summer's afternoon and the bees were buzzing noisily around the flowers that were in full bloom. A number of butterflies were fluttering around in the light breeze, something that Abigail found fascinating to watch. There was a large spider web on a rose bush, and she was doing her best to make sure that none of the silly little insects blundered their way into it.

"What're you doing?" an unexpected voice suddenly asked.

Abigail had turned round, her face full of childish happiness, only to find herself confronted by two boys glaring and frowning at her.

"Watching the bees!" she told them, pointing at the flowers. "Look, they're gathering pollen to make honey!"

The boys continued glaring at her with sullen expressions on their faces. Their fists were clenched and their shoulders were all hunched up, making them look like angry bears. Her smile faded and all thoughts about the spider web vanished from her mind.

"What's your full name?" demanded one of them.

"Abigail Nussbaum," she replied. Her voice trailed off at the end.

"That's a Jewish name. We don't like Jews,"

Abigail opened her mouth to say something but no words came out. One of the boys shoved her over, sending her falling to the ground. She looked up at them fearfully, knowing that they were going to hurt her again. Why were the boys - and it was *always* the boys - so mean to her? Was it because she was a girl? Was it because she was small?

"Jew, Jew. Smells of poo," they chanted at her.

Abigail felt her mouth twitch. She tried her hardest not to cry, but she knew the tears would come. The boys always knew how to make her cry and the boys would always hurt her when she cried.

"Jew, Jew. Flush it down the loo," they sang at her. "Jew, Jew. That is you."

Abigail heard a noise and her brother suddenly appeared from nowhere. His face was twisted up into a snarl and she could see that he was angry, angrier than she had ever seen him. At the time, she had thought that he was angry with her and she let out a small whimper.

Her brother's arm moved, and somehow one of the boys fell to the floor clutching the side of his head. Leo's foot moved and the boy let out a loud gasp as if all the air had been pushed out of his lungs. When Leo turned back around, the look on his face had scared her even more. He shouted something, causing the other boy to run away as fast as he could. When Leo looked down at Abigail, it sent a cold chill running through her. He bent down and she was aware of strong hands gripping her under her armpits. There was a sensation of being lifted into the air and she found herself being held up against his chest.

"If you ever touch my sister again, I'll kill you," a fierce voice growled next to her ear.

Her view of the world spun round and a hand was placed gently onto her back as Leo carried her away. "It's okay, Abbie. I'm here now. They won't hurt you again," the voice said.

Abigail put her arms around Leo's neck and buried her face into his shoulder. It was safe for her to cry now, as no-one was going to hurt her or say nasty things whilst her big, strong brother was here.

In the days that followed the incident, several things played on Abigail's mind. She knew that there was no way she could stand up to these boys, so she did what seemed to be the most logical thing - from then on, she always made sure that her hair was brushed, that she was clean, and that her clothes were neat and tidy. If she made sure that she didn't look Jewish, no-one would be able to pick on her for it; if she was the cleanest person in the class, no-one would be able to say that she smelled of poo.

As she replayed what had happened over and over again in her mind, Abigail realised that she was glad that Leo had hurt one of the boys. In fact, she wished that Leo had caught the other boy as well, instead of letting him get away. Her opportunities for revenge were few and far between, so she relished every morsel of justice that presented itself to her.

Lastly, she wanted to find some way of thanking Leo for helping her. However, each time she had tried speaking to him about it, she always became shy and embarrassed. In the end she decided to stick with what she was good at: making things. But what sort of thing could she possibly make that he would like? He certainly wouldn't be interested in daisy chains or pressed flowers. Luckily, she got some inspiration from an unlikely source - the school. During one of the classes, the teacher produced some stripped palm leaves and everyone was tasked with making something from them. Abigail had never seen them before, and she was fascinated with how smooth and flexible they felt in her hands. She watched as some of her classmates began making crucifixes, something that they had learnt to do at their local church. Abigail decided to copy them and soon enough she had a number of crosses laid out on the table in front of her. Although she had enjoyed making them, she wanted to try her hand at something more elaborate. She grabbed a handful of leaves and sat over in the corner of the classroom so she could work uninterrupted, and for the rest of the afternoon she remained there folding and weaving the leaves together into a pretty pattern. Although she had no real idea what it was that she was making, learning how to manipulate the exotic-looking palm leaves had been great fun.

Towards the end of the day, the teacher came over to her and asked to see what it was that she was making. Abigail had no real idea what it was, so just showed it to her.

"Abbie, that's wonderful!" exclaimed the teacher. "You've made a bookmark!"

When the teacher held it up to show the entire class, Abigail felt a surge of panic rush through her. She was worried that someone might take it away and rip it up, and when she got the bookmark back she stuffed it into her pocket to keep it safe.

When Abigail arrived back home, she sat down on her bed and looked at her new creation: it really *did* look like a bookmark. And that was when she knew she had something that Leo might like.

For the next two days it remained under her bed as she agonised over whether to give it to her brother or not. Although she knew he liked to read books, she didn't know if he wanted a bookmark from his silly little sister. What if he laughed at it? What if he tore it to pieces right there in front of her? On the day that she finally plucked up the courage to give it to him, Leo was sitting on his bed reading a book. She crept quietly into his room, startling him by appearing so suddenly in the corner of his eye. He put his book down and turned to face her.

"Hello, Abbie," he said.

She smiled nervously up at him, unsure of what to say. She brought the bookmark out from behind her back and placed it on his bed. For whatever reason, she thought that he was less likely to reject the gift if it wasn't actually in her hand at the time.

"I made you something. I hope you like it," she finally explained.

When he picked it up, a look of curious amusement had appeared on his face. For a painful moment, Abigail thought he was going to laugh at her and she felt herself shrinking back into her shell. Instead, he hugged her and thanked her for the present. She was thrilled that he knew it was a bookmark, and he even promised to start using it right away. A few days later Abigail's curiosity got the better of her and she dared a peek into Leo's room. A surge of relief and happiness ran through her when she saw the bookmark poking out from the bottom of his book.

The appearance of smoke rising up from the bombed out building brought Abigail back to the present day. A small shiver ran down her spine and she slid her hands into the pockets of her coat. Her fingers touched something soft and cold, and it took her a few moments to realise that it was the slice of bread she had taken from the soup kitchen. She took a bite and fought against the urge to wolf the entire thing down in one go. It might be the only food they had this evening, so she slid it back into her pocket.

For the next couple of hours, Abigail had to entertain herself as her mother slept. She went into the room she shared with Leo and looked under her bed. In amongst all her worldly possessions, the empty tin can from the night before stood taller and prouder than any of them. The juice from the peaches had dried, making it all sticky, so she took it over to the sink and washed it under the small trickle of water that dribbled out of the tap.

Also under her bed were some smooth pebbles that she had found out on the street some time ago. One of them had a small dimple in the middle of it that reminded her of the soap dish they had in their bathroom back home, and when she rolled them around in her hands the noise reminded her of when they used to play board games on the kitchen table. She always had to keep an eye out for her father's cheating during sessions of Snakes and Ladders or Ludo, and it was hard to decide what she enjoyed the most: winning a game, or loudly announcing when she caught him moving his pieces too far.

Abigail decided to re-arrange all the items so that they mimicked what her old room looked like back home. She took one of the empty cigarette packets and decided it was the perfect thing to represent her bed - if she bent the lid back, she could even pretend it had a headboard. When the faint smell of tobacco wafted under her nose, she immediately thought of fried potatoes. Although her parents weren't smokers, it seemed that almost everyone in her wider family was - whenever they went to family gatherings, the smell of cigarettes would hang heavily in the air. Abigail's fondness for fried potatoes was well-known and there would always be a small plate of them at the dinner table for her.

The small pebbles served a number of purposes in the recreation of her bedroom. One was used as a pillow, whilst the one with the straight edges was perfect as a chest of drawers. A short piece of string arranged into a small loop was ideal as a rug; another cigarette packet was used for her cupboard; an old button was the perfect shape for a bedside table.

Once she had finished remaking her bedroom, Abigail lay there on the floor with her chin resting on both hands. When she let out a small sigh, her breath sent a ball of dust rolling across the ground and she reached out to touch it. The soft, fluffy feel of the dust ball reminded her of their pet cat, so she placed it on top of the pretend bed and stroked it with her finger.

Later on that evening, Leo returned with another package under his arm. He placed it onto the table, unveiling half a loaf of bread and several strips of dried meat. Leo had no idea what type of meat it was and he was glad that no-one enquired about it -

sometimes it's better to make do with what's available, rather than risk getting squeamish about things. Using a knife, he cut the strips up into smaller pieces and shared them out.

Abigail tentatively put a chunk of the meat in her mouth. Although it had familiar taste, it was too chewy and stringy to be able tell what it was. The bread wasn't particularly soft or fresh, but at least it was edible - sometimes the bread would be so hard that it had to be soaked in water first. Much to everyone else's amusement, Abigail referred to this process as bringing the bread back to life.

"Me and Mum did some tidying and cleaning earlier," Abigail said conversationally.

Chana smiled when she saw the blank look on her son's face. "Let me guess, you didn't even notice?"

Abigail rolled her eyes. "Boys," she muttered, shaking her head.

Leo let out a small laugh.

"Don't worry, we didn't touch your bed," his mother reassured him. "We know you like it the way you have it."

The three of them let the rest of the private joke remain unspoken. It wasn't the first time that someone had pointed out that Leo's bed back home was almost as untidy as the one he had here in the ghetto.

"How've you been feeling today?" Leo asked his mother.

"Better, much better," she replied. "I had to have a lie down earlier, but the feeling of exhaustion has gone. I don't know what's been the matter with me, I really don't."

Leo nodded in reply but didn't say anything. He had a pretty good idea what had caused her to feel so ill for such a long period of time. The death of their father had hit both Abigail and himself hard, but they had ways of dealing with it. Abigail had her own little private dream world that she could retreat into when things got out of hand, whilst Leo had been lucky enough to find some friends who were supportive and offered him plenty of channels to direct his anger into. Their mother had neither of those things so had been forced to bear the burden all by herself.

"I'm hoping to go and help out down at that soup kitchen tomorrow," Chana reminded them.

"Okay, that's good," Leo told her. "Some of the volunteers don't last very long, so they need all the help they can get."

Out the corner of his eye, Leo could see that Abigail was looking at him. He knew that she was keen to help out in some way, but he hated the thought of her being out in the ghetto when he wasn't there to keep her safe. However, he also knew that it was unfair to expect her to sit up here in this grubby little apartment all day by herself. Ultimately, what was worse - risking his sister's life by letting her out, or risking her sanity by keeping her locked up? Leo stared down at the table until Abigail wasn't looking at him anymore - he had no answers to any of the questions that she might ask him.

As the evening wore on, the room gradually became darker and darker. It wasn't quite as cold as it had been the night before, so Abigail decided to sleep in her own bed this time. Although they hadn't been able to clean the sheets, the tidying up that they had done earlier in the day at least allowed her to pretend that things were nice and pristine. There was also the new bedroom under her bed to keep her feeling warm and cosy. When she closed her eyes, she could almost smell the pleasant aroma of fresh linen and as she drifted off to sleep, she could practically feel the soft footsteps of their cat jumping up onto her bed.

"Night, Tabby," Abigail whispered.

\*\*\*

# Chapter 3

The next morning, Chana was the first to wake up. She lay still for a while, allowing herself to drift in and out of a light doze. There was a crack in the wall to the left of her bed, one that had been there ever since they first arrived. Chana was sure that it was becoming gradually longer and wider as time went on, leading her to wonder what had caused it. Was it just one more secret weapon that the Germans were using to make their lives worse? Was someone digging an escape tunnel somewhere underneath them? Or was it just her mind playing tricks on her?

She got up out of bed and ran her fingers along the crack. The bare plaster was cold and unwelcoming, almost as if it resented her being there. Chana couldn't feel a draught coming through the gap, so she hoped it was merely superficial damage - the cold winters were already bad enough without having to worry about the walls crumbling down around them.

She walked out of her room and into the main living area. The bare, unpolished table and featureless chairs stood empty and silent before her. It was like looking at a display of old, excavated skeletons rather than a place that a family could sit and have their meals. The chairs that she and Abigail had been sitting on last night were tucked neatly under the table, whilst Leo's was poking out at an angle. It glared back at Chana, almost as if it had been caught trying to escape.

At one point there had been enough chairs for the entire family to sit on - where had the fourth one gone? Had it been burnt for warmth? Traded for a loaf of bread? She couldn't remember and didn't want to remember.

Her eyes flicked over to a corner of the room. There was nothing there other than dust and bare floorboards yet it was a spot that terrified her. Although it pained her to admit it, she was glad that Mr Karski was no longer with them. She had no idea what his fate had been and she didn't want to know: she just didn't want him here in the same place with her.

She remembered one particular day when she returned from the market. As she walked in through the door, she spied Mr Karski coming out of her bedroom and it had sent a cold chill running down her spine. She hated the way he was so tall; hated the way he had to dip his head whenever he went through the doorways; hated the way he seemed to take up so much space. What had he been doing in her bedroom? What on earth was in there that was any of his business? Why couldn't he just find somewhere else to sleep?

A small sound to her right caused her to snap her head round. It came from the bedroom that Leo and Abigail shared, and she crept over to the doorway. There was no movement from either of them, but she guessed it had been her daughter shifting in her sleep.

Chana stepped inside and approached Abigail's bed. She held her breath, not wanting to wake her delicate little girl up, and stood there watching her for a few minutes. In the gloom it took her a few moments to spot the slight rise and fall of her chest. She reached out and touched her daughter carefully on the shoulder, knowing that the wrong type of disturbance could wake her. Back in their old home, Chana had often marvelled at how Abigail could remain fast asleep as the cat walked across her bed, only to wake up if someone made a noise in another room of the house.

Chana thought about how utterly unfair it was for someone like Abigail to be caught up in this stupid war; it was almost impossible to imagine a more innocent child. If she ever saw someone try to swat a fly with a rolled up newspaper, Abigail would frown and shake her head at them. She had even cried in her room for nearly two whole days after she found out what happened to unwanted kittens on a farm.

Chana felt a sudden urge to slip into the bed and hold her daughter close to her.

"Mum? You alright?"

The unexpected sound of her son's voice startled her and she flinched round to face him.

"Yes, I... I was just watching her. She looks so..." she shrugged and didn't finish the sentence.

Leo nodded at her. After sleeping in the same room as his sister for so long, he knew what his mother was talking about. Whilst he hadn't ever stood there like his mother had done, he would sometimes glance at Abigail and be struck by how peaceful she looked.

Half an hour later, all three of them were awake and Abigail was standing in her usual place by the window. Leo was sitting in his chair at the table, yawning and scratching at his head. Chana paced around restlessly, feeling nervous about going out.

"We may as well go to the soup kitchen again," said Leo. "It's the only way we'll be getting something to eat this morning."

Abigail wrinkled her nose but didn't say anything. Although she had enjoyed being in the room with all those other people, the man at the door gave her the creeps.

Chana looked at her son. "We may as well get going now."

As they trooped down the stairs, Leo smiled to himself as he saw Abigail peering down at what she thought was a mouse hole.

The sound of a large vehicle bore down on them once they were out on the street. The three of them hugged the side of the building, and a few seconds later a military truck roared past them. Abigail frowned as it disappeared into the distance, wondering why they always drove so fast down these narrow streets - if someone had been standing in the road, it wouldn't have been able to stop in time.

They turned a corner and came to an area that opened up into what might once have been a pleasant courtyard. A few rough holes in the ground suggested that some trees had once been planted here for decorative purposes. Hard times meant that they had been dug up and used for firewood. Next to a wall, two crude tents had been erected using planks of wood, rope, and a number of flimsy, sagging sheets. A young boy stood outside one of them, looking morosely at the people who were walking past his makeshift home. A length of barbed wire was being used to dry laundry.

Abigail was struck by the strange sight of a lone bed standing next to a building. Two pillows and a blanket lay in a crumpled heap on top of it.

"What happens when it rains?" Abigail wondered aloud.

"It gets wet," Leo informed her.

Half a dozen questions popped into Abigail's head. She wanted to know whose bed it was and how had it got there. What was going to happen to it? Why was everyone walking past it as if it was perfectly normal for a bed to be dumped there?

They turned into another street, just in time to see a German soldier raise his hand and point at someone on the other side of the road.

"Hey!" the soldier shouted. "Where's your permit?"

Several people turned round, whilst others simply put their heads down and hurried along. The man that the soldier was pointing at froze, and a chasm seemed to open up around him as everyone scurried away to safety.

"Permit! Now!" the soldier bellowed at him.

The man fumbled nervously around in his pockets and brought out a few flimsy bits of paper. The soldier swatted the man's arm aside, sending them fluttering to the ground like discarded autumn leaves.

"Show me your permit!" the soldier screamed at the man, who was now scrambling around in the dirt.

Abigail watched this unfolding with abject horror. She wasn't entirely sure what a permit was or why the soldier would want to see one, but she guessed that it had something to do with the pieces of paper that had been in the man's pocket. Maybe a permit was like an invitation, or like the ticket you had to show at the gate when you went to the circus.

"Permit!" the soldier repeated. He unhooked a truncheon from his belt and tapped it impatiently in the palm of his hand.

Abigail's horror turned into confusion. How could the soldier not see what the man was doing? She wanted to run up and tell him that the permit was there, right there on the ground in front of him. Could he not see the bits of paper? He should be quick, otherwise they'll get soaked and dirty in the mud.

The soldier hit the man in the back, who yelled in pain and fell to the floor.

"Permit!"

Abigail gasped and raised a hand to her mouth. Why was the soldier so angry? If the man doesn't have the right permit, why not just ask him to go home and get it? Why not put up a sign so that people know what permit is needed?

The soldier hit the man again and shouted at him once more. Abigail thought it was like watching an absurd routine at the circus, where everything was deliberately over the top and the clowns hit each other over the head with metal poles. The only difference was that no-one was laughing.

"Permit!"

*Whack.*

"Permit!"

*Whack.*

"Permit!"

*Whack.*

By now the man had stopped moving and his hair was matted with a thick dark liquid, whilst a red goo was beginning to ooze down his forehead. The soldier calmly secured his truncheon back onto his belt and remained still for a few moments. He stood there breathing deeply, as if he was a boy messenger trying to catch his breath back so he could dutifully recite what he had to say. A handkerchief appeared from out of his pocket and wiped the sweat from his brow.

A cold chill ran through Abigail when she saw the soldier point his pistol down at the man who was now lying unconscious on the ground. The beginnings of a scream stirred somewhere in her midsection, and she was utterly powerless as it shot up through her chest and filled her throat. She opened her mouth, took a deep breath, her eyes wide with terror, her fingers balling themselves into tight fists, before a big strong hand appeared from nowhere and clamped itself over her mouth. Abigail's throat was filled with the taste of dirt, grime, and sweat, and she knew that this was it. This was going to be the day when she got beaten with a stick because she didn't have a ticket for the circus.

The soldier pulled the trigger of the pistol and the street was filled with a loud noise. Abigail flinched and wondered why the man's head had changed shape all of a sudden. His face looked as if it had been replaced with something that belonged on the floor of a butcher's shop.

A hand grabbed at the back of her coat and pushed her away. She caught a quick glimpse of her mother looking grave and worried, before another hand grabbed at her and she felt herself being lifted and pulled around a corner. When she turned back around, she was surprised to see Leo standing there in front of her. Although his face was dirty she could see how pale he looked underneath the grime. Her mother was leaning against a wall with her head in her hands.

A paralysing numbness ran through Abigail and she decided to stay where she was until someone told her what to do. She closed her eyes and retreated back into her little dream world, and it wasn't long before images of flowers, trees, and birds flashed before her. There was a sensation of floating and for a split second she thought she was back home in her bed.

When she opened her eyes again, both her mother and Leo were looking at her.

"You okay?" Leo asked. "We thought you'd fallen asleep."

Abigail nodded and noticed that the colour had returned to her brother's face.

"Come on, let's get going," he said.

They arrived at the same building as before and quickly checked to make sure that no-one was watching them. Leo knocked on the door and said something to the scruffy face that peered out at them.

"My mother wants to volunteer to help out down there," Leo said once they were all inside.

The man coughed loudly, causing Abigail to wonder if he was sick. He looked Chana over and nodded. "Okay, fair enough. But she'll need to come back later, it's busy at the moment. Word gets around fast. Go and grab something to eat, then come back in a few hours."

The three of them went down the stairs and saw for themselves just how busy it was. The queue was longer this time, almost to the door. The serving of soup they received wasn't as large as it had been the day before and they weren't given as much butter with their bread either. Abigail also had to make do with one of the larger spoons again.

There weren't enough seats for them to sit together, so they had to make do whenever a space became available. Abigail sat between two old men and thought back to the discarded slice of bread she had found the day before. It made her feel wary about leaving her own bit of bread on the table, in case someone took it when she wasn't looking. After taking a large bite, she discretely slipped it into her coat pocket.

As she worked her way through her meal, Abigail stole glances at the people around her. Some of them seemed to be eating too quickly, causing them to spill the food back into the bowl. Others were holding their spoons like Leo did, grasping it in their fist as if they were wielding a club. She remembered the way her mother used to scold Leo for not holding his cutlery properly - he'd roll his eyes and comply with her request, only to change his grip again when she wasn't looking. There was one particular time when he got sent upstairs to his room for it, and after the meal was finished Abigail decided to sneak some food up to him. She grabbed a bowl and filled it with a couple of roast potatoes, a slice of meat, and two scoops of chocolate ice cream. They were his favourite foods so it seemed like a logical choice, but when she took it up to him he had howled with laughter. It turned out that she had forgotten to even bring him a spoon or a fork and she flushed red with embarrassment. Leo decided to share it with her, and she sat cross-legged on his bed as he showed her how to use a bit of chicken to eat the ice cream.

The man sitting to the left of Abigail began coughing. When she saw that he wasn't going to cover his mouth, she suddenly felt trapped and claustrophobic. She shifted away from him and dragged her bowl closer to her chest, as did some of the others who were sitting around her. She looked around for Leo or her mother but couldn't see either of them anywhere and their absence made the room seem less inviting than it had been the day before. The walls didn't feel as protective, the paint looked as if it was all cracked and peeling, whilst the pipes and light fittings that crisscrossed the ceiling seemed flimsier and rustier. In fact, some of the pipes didn't even seem to go anywhere and it was like looking at a maze of jumbled metal that looped back in on itself. Was it all part of another German trick?

Abigail thought back to some of the trips she had taken to the local theatre in their hometown. The way the sets could be changed over so quickly and convincingly had fascinated and thrilled her. The presence of a few windows and a wall could transform the entire stage into a street, whilst a single tree and a green spotlight could whisk you away to a dense forest. If the local drama group was capable of such things, heaven only knew what the Germans could do.

Abigail finished her bowl of soup and carefully placed her spoon to signify that she had finished. She glanced around again but still couldn't see either her mother or Leo anywhere. Had they rejoined the queue for a second helping? Had they left and forgotten about her? Had they been thrown out?

There was some jostling somewhere to her right as people shifted their chairs to let someone squeeze in behind them. She could feel someone standing right behind her, and she just knew it was a boy. It was always the boys who made her feel afraid and this time they were here to tell her to get out of the seat, or to reclaim that bit of bread that she had taken the day before. Maybe it was Mr Karski returning to ask why she never spoke to him.

A grubby hand appeared from nowhere and slammed a bowl down in front of her. Soup slopped up and around the sides, spilling precious morsels of meat and potato onto the table.

Abigail remained still, hoping against hope that if she didn't move the man would go away. She stared intently at her spoon, now noticing that the handle wasn't straight - there was a strange kink where someone had bent it out of shape and then tried to level it out again. Some of the boys did this in the canteen at school, and she noticed that it was usually done by the boys who picked on her for being small or Jewish. She couldn't understand why they were so outraged with her being smelly, yet had no qualms about breaking the things that other people used.

Abigail flinched when a strong hand grabbed her by the shoulder. She closed her eyes, readying herself to be picked up out of the chair and dumped outside where all the soldiers were.

"Here," said a voice. "It's all I could get for a second helping, there's not as much to go around today."

The grubby hand let go of the new bowl and picked up her empty one. She followed the arm up to the shoulder and relief swept over her when she found the familiar face of Leo. An awkward lump gathered in her throat, one that seemed impossible to swallow back down.

"We can't stay for too long either, it's getting busier," he told her.

Abigail nodded but didn't say anything. Leo seemed to notice the glistening in her eyes and placed a comforting hand on her head.

"Don't worry, I'm keeping an eye on you. Just stand up when you're finished and I'll come and get you."

When he turned and disappeared from Abigail's view, she took the remains of the bread from her pocket and finished it quickly. The bowl Leo had brought her was only half full but she was relieved that he had managed to find her one of the smaller spoons.

Once she had finished, Abigail set her spoon straight and looked at the people around her: she didn't recognise any of them and it was as if everyone she had initially sat down with had been secretly replaced without her noticing. Remembering what Leo told her, she stood up and spotted him waving at her through a small gap between two people. She headed towards him, doing her best to squeeze in between everyone. As she twisted round to fit through a rapidly-closing gap, she bumped against a protruding elbow. There was a loud clatter of cutlery on metal and the sound of someone cursing loudly. Before she could even think about apologising, Leo reached out and pulled her through the crowd. He grabbed her hand and gestured for her to follow him. When they reached the bottom of the stairs, their mother was standing there waiting for them and she puffed her cheeks out and smiled with relief when she caught sight of her daughter.

"Everything okay? It's rammed in there, we thought we'd never find you!" she said.

"Yes, Leo kept me safe," Abigail replied.

On the way back up the stairs they had to squeeze past some people going down. Chana checked with the man at the door about coming back later.

"Sure, we could do with an extra pair of hands," he told her. "At the rate they're coming in we're going to have to start turning people away soon." He saw the grave look on her face. "Either that, or we just feed everyone a bowl of water," he explained.

Leo led them out of the door and they made their way back to the apartment. Before they had gone very far, Abigail suddenly stopped in the middle of the road. A look of curiosity appeared on her face and she turned her head slowly to the left.

Leo glanced back at her and felt a rush of annoyance run through him. What on earth was she playing at? An hour ago they had watched someone get shot, and here she is playing games in the middle of the street. He opened his mouth to say something... and closed it again. His face took on a bewildered expression.

Chana frowned, wondering what was going on between them. Although her two children were very different, it wasn't uncommon for them to have their shared moments together. They squabbled and argued as all siblings do, but there were times when they would suddenly look at each other and laugh, almost as if they were sharing the same private joke.

Abigail looked back at Leo and was surprised to see that he was tilting his head to one side.

"Can you hear it as well?" she asked him.

"Yeah," he replied. "But what is it?"

Although Abigail had a good idea what it was that they were hearing, it seemed too absurd to be true. It was a sound that conjured up memories of carousels, candy floss, and laughter. It reminded her of a time when the only reason you might be hungry at bedtime was if you had been sent upstairs for misbehaving. It reminded her of when soldiers were honourable men that you read about in books but never actually got to see.

"What's what?" asked Chana. She sounded confused and alarmed.

"It's... fairground music," Abigail told her, not quite able to believe it herself.

The three of them stood there dumbstruck for a few moments.

"How? Where? What do you mean?" Chana asked.

"It's fairground music," Leo confirmed.

Leo began walking in the direction of where the music was coming from. Although Abigail wanted to follow him, she was afraid of what they might find. What if it was another German trick? What if this road led to the top of a large hill, one that was so steep that they couldn't walk back? What if a gigantic hole had been dug in the ground, ready to swallow them up and bury them alive? What if there was nothing at the end of the road but soldiers and truncheons?

Leo turned around and gestured for them to follow him. "Let's take a look," he decided. "What's the worst that can happen?"

For the next five minutes they followed the music. It gradually became louder and louder, until it was almost clanging in their ears like a monstrous set of church bells. The streets became familiar and a flush of anger ran through Leo as he realised what was going on. They turned a final corner and found themselves staring at a solid brick wall that stretched as far as the eye could see in both directions.

Abigail looked up at the wall until her head was craning to see the top of it. When she took a step back to get a better look, ugly coils of barbed wire popped into view. They glared down at her and for a moment Abigail thought that the music was being blasted out from the spikes that ran along the wire. She reached out and touched the wall, not quite believing that it was actually there. Although she had heard about it, this was the first time she had actually seen the Ghetto Wall with her own eyes. She listened carefully and underneath the loud music she could hear the unmistakeable sounds of people laughing and having fun. Whilst she and her family were locked inside this horrendous place, those on the other side of the wall were stepping onto merry-go-rounds, bobbing for apples, and throwing wooden hoops to try and win a goldfish. Abigail closed her eyes and put her ear up against the brickwork. It was cold, hard, and uncompromising, and she couldn't sense any of the happiness that was going on over the other side. Did those people even know what was going on so close to them? Did they care? Was the funfair there so they could have fun, or so they could drown out the suffering that was happening right on their doorstep?

Leo clenched his fists and gritted his teeth. He remembered when the wall was first built, having often watched the workers from a distance - every grain of cement and every single brick had been laid by Jewish hands. At first the Germans had kept them under close guard, but they soon got bored when they realised how compliant the workers were willing to be in sealing their own fate. Leo had pleaded with them to sabotage it in some way - to mix something in with the cement to weaken it, or to dig holes underneath where they were laying the bricks - but to no effect. They were either scared of upsetting the Germans, or more concerned with getting an extra ration of bread for being good little Jewish workers. Some of the workers had even ganged up on him after his pleading turned abusive.  Like most Jewish boys, Leo had learnt how to fight at an early age but even he knew that five against one was only going to go one way.

There was a break in the music and when Leo glanced around he saw that dozens of other people had gathered nearby, all of them staring up at the wall.  At least one person could be heard sobbing.

"How can you just forget us?" someone yelled up at the barbed wire.  "How can you go to the fair while we starve?"

The music quickly started up again, once again drowning out the sounds of misery completely.

Abigail spotted something at the foot of the wall and bent down to pick it up.  It was a discarded lump of cement and there were curious swirls running across it that made it look like a marble.  She slipped it into her pocket.

Chana looked down at her feet.  "How long are we going to be in this horrible place for?" she asked.

"Not for much longer," Leo said to no-one in particular.  "Not for much longer."

Abigail looked up at him with a curious frown.

***

# Chapter 4

When they arrived back at the apartment, Leo was the first one to step inside. They didn't have a key to lock either of the doors so there was always the lingering worry about what they might be coming back to. Leo glanced quickly around the room to see if anything was missing. Although they didn't have anything of real value, it was funny how things were sometimes - he had seen people start arguments and fights over something as simple as a shoelace. Probably his biggest fear was coming back to find another family settling in and making themselves at home. Leo had often asked himself what he would do if something like that happened. Would he throw them out into the streets, putting them at the mercy of the elements and the soldiers? Or would he grudgingly welcome them in, giving them free use of Mr Karski's old corner?

Abigail looked at the lump of cement she had picked up. Some of the edges had disintegrated, and she turned her pocket inside out to get rid of the loose grains.

Chana yawned. "I'm going to have a quick lie down," she announced and disappeared into her room.

Two hours later, the sound of a German truck rumbling down the road woke Chana up. She lay there listening to it disappear off into the distance, wondering where it was going and for what purpose. Exactly what did they need those trucks for? Was it for bringing food in? Had the war finally ended and the supply lines were being opened up? Or were they just transporting soldiers around because their shifts had changed? What if the trucks were being used to move people? Chana didn't want to think about what the destination might be if that was the case.

A small cough and a giggle drifted in through the bedroom doorway. Chana swung her legs out of bed and put her feet flat on the floor; it was as cold and as hard as it always was. She slipped into her shoes and walked out into the main room of the apartment. For a moment she thought she was still dreaming and she blinked a few times to make sure she was actually awake. Sitting at the table were Leo and Abigail, having what appeared to be an arm wrestling competition. Leo's face was contorted with exaggerated strain, whilst Abigail giggled as she used both hands to push her older brother's arm ever closer to the table. Leo let his arm collapse onto the table and his tongue flopped out of his mouth in mock exhaustion, sending Abigail into fits of laughter.

Chana rubbed her eyes and felt a wave of sadness run through her. It was like seeing them at the dinner table back home, waiting for their supper. She remembered when Leo once hid Abigail's cutlery under her seat cushion, and then told her off for not laying the table properly. When she went off to the kitchen, he hid her glass behind the vase of flowers that had been placed in the middle of the table. On her return, Abigail's face was a picture of confusion as she began to wonder if she was going mad. Leo had rolled his eyes at her and told her to sit down before her dinner went cold. To her credit, Abigail saw the funny side when she discovered why her seat was so lumpy.

"I'll be off soon," Chana announced. "Hopefully things have died down at the kitchen by now."

Leo glanced up and nodded. "Yeah, you'll be okay to go there now," he reassured her.

Chana went into the small bathroom and tried the taps. Although she wasn't likely to be doing much more than cleaning tables and chopping vegetables, her anxiety made her feel as if she was going for an important job interview somewhere in the city. There was a small bit of relief when she discovered that the water was working, allowing her to have a quick wash.

"Wish me luck," she told Leo and Abigail when she was ready to go.

"Good luck," they chimed in unison.

As she made her way down the stairs, her shoes sounded disturbingly loud on the coarse concrete steps. She glanced down at the small hole in the wall and wondered if anyone was using it to spy on her. The door that led out into the street creaked loudly as she opened it, and a soft breeze prompted her to button her coat up. Chana made her way along the streets, doing her best to avoid looking directly at any of the soldiers standing guard on the corners. She wondered exactly what it was that they were actually supposed be guarding. It had been the Germans who had forced them to come here in the first place - surely the easiest way to make sure no-one misbehaved themselves was to let everyone go back to their old homes.

At one point the roads and the buildings began to look all the same, and she began to worry that she was lost. She peered through the gaps in between the larger buildings, desperately searching for anything that she might recognise. The orphanage was a tall building and was one of the more prominent landmarks around here, yet she couldn't find it. Chana tried to suppress the unmistakeable feeling that this was all part of another German trick. She wondered if any of the buildings around her were actually real - if she touched the walls would it be bricks she felt underneath her fingers, or the soft canvas of a painted stage prop? As she quickened her pace, the echo of her footsteps made it sound as if she were being followed. Again, was this all part of a German trick? Was someone standing just round the corner, banging two shoes together?

Chana spotted a partially collapsed building and felt relieved when she realised where she was. After glancing around to make sure that no-one was looking, she headed towards the entrance of the soup kitchen and knocked on the door. Something moved in the corner of her vision, but she couldn't see anything when she stepped back to take a closer look. As she turned her head back round, she nearly yelped in fright when she saw an eye peering at her through a crack in the door.

"Hello, I'm Chana. I spoke to someone this morning about helping out and they told me to come back later."

For a split second Chana thought that she was literally talking to a floating eye. It closed and then opened up again, sending a cold shiver down her spine. There was the sound of a sliding chain and the door began to swing open, exposing the same scruffy face that she had seen earlier.

"Come on in," the man said. "It's all empty now but there's plenty to do still. Go on down, they're expecting you."

Chana nodded at him but didn't say any more. The man had an odd gruffness about him that unsettled her, and if this was how he acted towards people who were helping out she hoped that she never saw him when he had to turn people away. As she made her way along the corridor and down the steps towards the basement, she was certain that things looked different this time around. The ceiling seemed a bit lower, the walls seemed closer

49

together, and there were dirty cobwebs lurking in nearly every corner.

Chana walked through the final doorway and stepped into the large room. Empty tables and chairs stared silently back at her, almost as if she had interrupted some kind of secret furniture meeting.

"Hello, you must Chana," said a voice to her left.

A woman seemed to appear from nowhere and introduced herself with a warm smile. "I'm Kasia, pleased to meet you."

Chana shook the woman's hand and did her best to return the smile. She was feeling flustered and unsure of herself, suddenly aware that she had barely spoken to another soul for the last few months. It was as if she had been in a coma and the world had moved on without her.

"Come on, I'll introduce you to everyone else," Kasia told her. "We're having a bit of a break at the moment. There's cake and tea if you want some."

Chana blinked, convinced that she had misheard. Kasia saw the surprised look on the newcomer's face and smiled. She touched her gently on the arm and led her into a large kitchen area.

Pots, pans, and bowls were stacked up in the sinks, whilst the middle of the room was dominated by four tables that had been arranged into a single work surface. A plate with what looked to be a fruit cake - *cake!* - on it stood near one edge and a large teapot covered with a knitted green tea cosy lay nearby. Three women in chairs surrounded this mini feast and they all looked up at the same time. Kasia introduced Chana and pulled up a chair for her. A fresh cup and a small plate appeared before her, and were promptly filled up in the blink of an eye.

Chana thanked them and sat down, still feeling somewhat bewildered. It was like she had been transported back home and was having afternoon tea with her friends. Her hand trembled slightly as she picked up a slice of cake and bit into it. Almost instantly her mouth was filled with a glorious sweetness that she had forgotten even existed. Her taste buds opened up like flowers on the first day of spring and her tongue embraced the cake as if it were being reunited with a long lost friend. Chana's hand and throat began pushing and pulling in unison, like two smugglers carrying a treasure chest down into a secret basement.

She swallowed hard, just about managing to avoid choking herself. Her eyes watered and she blinked rapidly to clear her vision.

"I'm sorry, where are my manners?" she apologised. "It's just... well, you know..."

The women looked at her sympathetically.

"Been a long time since you had a treat?" one of them asked. "Don't worry, I've only been here a few days. I did the same thing as you."

Chana took a deep breath and composed herself. She took a sip of tea and finished off the cake. Another slice instantly appeared in its place. She reached out and stroked the tea cosy, relishing the soft feel of the wool under her fingers.

"Home comforts," Kasia said. "It's amazing the difference they can make."

"It really is," Chana agreed. "Who knitted the cosy?"

There was a moment of silence before anyone answered.

"Someone who's no longer with us."

This brought Chana back to reality. She took another bite of cake, this time realising that it was actually rather dry and lacking in sugar. It tasted like the sort of thing Leo might end up baking if Abigail wasn't there to make sure he used the correct ingredients. Chana sat there chatting with the other ladies for the next two hours and they all seemed to have their own tragic story to tell.

"We were only given a day's notice and then we were dragged out of our homes."

"I came here with my husband and two girls. Now it's just me."

"We were crammed into a single room with another family. I don't know what happened to them though, haven't seen them for weeks."

"My daughter is very sick. I don't think she'll last much longer."

After a while Chana relaxed and found herself able to discuss her own situation for the first time. Once she started talking she found herself unable to stop, and ended up telling them everything. She recounted how helpless she felt as her husband's health slowly deteriorated until he wasn't much more than an ashen-faced figure lying in bed all day. There were no doctors and no medicine was available from anywhere. Partway through telling her story Chana burst into tears. They weren't just tears of grief, but tears of relief as well - simply being able to talk about it meant a huge burden had been lifted from her shoulders.

Once the tea and cake had all been finished, the ladies took it as their cue to get back to work. Several sacks of potatoes, carrots, and onions were dragged out from a storage room. Chana decided she would try to avoid dealing with the onions if she could - as far as she was concerned, she had done enough crying for one day already. She was soon busy peeling and chopping up the carrots, whilst someone else washed the remainder of the bowls and the cutlery. Initially Chana couldn't resist turning on the sink taps just because she could - having running hot water was something of a novelty these days. Chana also couldn't resist popping the occasional bit of carrot into her mouth as she worked her way through the pile. Kasia caught her in the act and shot her a friendly wink, causing a bashful grin to spread across Chana's face.

The vegetables were all thrown into large metal pots and placed onto the gas stoves to boil. Some large slabs of meat were brought out from the storage room and chopped up into small squares, whilst the fat was trimmed off and set to one side.

"We can't always get hold of meat," Kasia told Chana. "We'll fry those spare strips of fat separately so we can take them home."

The rest of the day was filled with cooking, cleaning, and making sure that everything was ready for when people started queuing up again. They managed to grab themselves a short break, just enough time for another cup of tea and a sit down. They remained in their chairs until the sound of footsteps coming down the stairs spurred them back into life. Although the day had so far been physically challenging for Chana, it was nothing that she hadn't done before. As a proud housewife she was more than used to doing endless amounts of cooking and cleaning - the only difference here had been the sheer amount of it.

However, none of that had prepared her for the mental challenge that lay ahead of her. At first people came in a trickle which was easy to deal with. She gave them a generous helping of soup, smiled pleasantly and told them to enjoy their meal. As time wore on, the place became busier and the faces seemed to become more haunted and desperate. A frail old man who struggled to hold onto his bowl spilled half the contents onto the floor, but no-one offered to help him as they didn't want to lose their place in the queue. A heavily pregnant woman was left to stand in a corner as all the seats were taken. After a while they had to reduce the size of the helpings they dished out so that there would be enough to go around, and Chana began to see the ghosts of her own family. In the eyes of every young girl she saw Abigail, whilst in every furrowed brow and square jaw line she saw Leo. After a while the desperate faces became too much and she had to avoid their gazes entirely.

By the time the evening was over, the ladle was like a lump of heavy lead and her shoulder was little more than a dull ache at the top of her arm. The bowls and cooking pots were gathered together before being rinsed out and left to dry overnight. Kasia brought out a smaller pot of soup and dished it out amongst them - there was just enough for two bowls each and they all ate eagerly.

"What time do you want me back tomorrow?" Chana asked.

"Same time as today if you want."

"You sure? Who's going to do the morning shift?"

Kasia smiled at her. "No-one does an entire day if we can help it. You did well today, make sure you get a good night's sleep."

When they all stepped outside to go back home, Chana was surprised to see that it was getting dark. They had been so busy down in the kitchen that it didn't seem like a whole day had passed. She said her goodbyes and set off back to the apartment. Although the work had worn her out, Chana was feeling more than pleased with herself. It felt good to finally do something other than lie in bed all day, and the other ladies were friendly and welcoming. They could sit down and have some tea and a chat when there was time, and the extra food meant she didn't have to worry about going hungry. In a way, life was almost back to normal.

Almost.

The roar of a German truck served as a stark reminder of where she was. She looked back over her shoulder and saw the headlights of a large vehicle turning into the road. Chana fought back the urge to run and instead ducked into a dark doorway. The truck roared on towards her, quickly accelerating up to a speed that was far too dangerous for a residential area such as this. She shrank as far back into the doorway as she could, desperately hoping that she hadn't been spotted. As it bore down on her, she closed her eyes and found herself consumed with the feeling that the truck was driving straight at her. She flung her eyes open again, only to be dazzled by the bright headlights that filled her vision. Just as they powered on past her, the loud squeal of a vehicle slamming on its brakes sent her heart thumping with fear. Although the engine was still running she heard the sound of a door being opened, followed by loud aggressive voices and then the door was slammed shut again. She heard heavy footsteps, footsteps that could only be made by someone strong, someone who could tear her apart without even trying; footsteps that belonged to someone wearing big black boots that could do terrible damage to a person and they became louder and louder until they seemed to stop right next to her. The throbbing sound of a diesel engine belching out poisonous exhaust fumes was loud and aggressive in her ears.

A strange tinkling sound reached her, one that started off faint and gradually increased in volume. She heard someone gasp with relief, followed by a strong smell of urine that made her gag. The tinkling stopped and the loud footsteps started up again, this time moving away from her. Chana heard the sound of a door opening and then being slammed shut again. As the truck roared back into life, she peered out to make sure it was really going away. An arm suddenly snaked out of the passenger window and fired a pistol down a side street. Chana flinched and ducked back into the doorway, her heart pounding with fear and she remained still until the noise of the vehicle had faded away completely.

Chana glanced around, realising that it was now almost entirely pitch black. She darted out of her hiding place and began making her way back to the apartment, not quite daring to lift her head up. What if there was a soldier lying in wait for her? She would be powerless to stop him from hurting her, powerless to stop

54

him from using his fists, from ripping the flimsy clothes from her back and doing what he wanted. When she walked past the road that the soldier had fired his gun down, Chana closed her eyes. The soldier might have been drunk and firing for the fun of it. Then again, he might have been firing at someone who was walking home. Chana didn't know and she didn't want to know.

The dark streets and empty alleyways seemed unfamiliar and threatening. She desperately tried to retread her journey to the soup kitchen in reverse, never entirely sure if she was doubling back on herself or not. A faint smell of burning reached her nose and she followed it, hoping that it was coming from the mysterious bombed out building. Relief swept through her as she turned a corner and recognised where she was. Although her hand closed eagerly around the doorknob to the apartment, for a split second she wondered what she was going to find inside. What if the entire thing was another German trick? What if the soup kitchen was part of an elaborate plan to get her out of the house? What if there were soldiers and dogs lying in wait for her, ready to pulverise her with their batons and sharp teeth?

She took a deep breath, pushed open the door and stepped inside. The room was gloomy, a stark change to the brightly-lit soup kitchen she had spent all day in. A candle in the middle of the table was the only source of light and it created a bubble of luminosity around itself. Leo and Abigail were both seated at the table and they were staring intently back at her. Chana realised that as she worried about who was inside the apartment, they too would have been concerned about who was coming up the stairs.

"Oh, thank God you're back!" exclaimed Leo. "We've been really worried ever since it began to get dark."

In the candlelight, Leo's grubby face made him look like a brave tribesman from the Middle East.

"How was it, Mum?" asked Abigail. "Did you get on alright?"

In contrast to her brother, Abigail's pale and pristine face seemed to glow in the candlelight. She looked beautiful and delicate like an angel. In between the two of them was half a loaf of bread. There were small pits and holes in the centre, as if two hungry people had been picking and nibbling at it whilst they waited for someone to come home. Chana smiled at them, the aches in her arms and hands temporarily forgotten.

"Yes, it was good," she said as she sat down. "Well, it was terrible seeing so many people like that. But it was good to do something for them."

"Are you going back tomorrow?" Abigail enquired.

"Yes. There's no way I could just abandon them like that," replied her mother. A small grin spread across her face. "Besides, they've got tea and cake."

Leo and Abigail's faces held a mixture of disbelief and surprise, making her feel guilty about indulging on the perks she had enjoyed earlier. Chana realised that she was probably the only one to have eaten since the morning.

"Here, I brought us something back," she said, putting a hand into her coat pocket.

Chana set a small bundle onto the table and unwrapped the cloth. Inside were the fried bits of meat fat that had been set aside earlier in the afternoon. Leo got a knife and cut them up into smaller pieces and shared them out. Chana took two bits and refused any more. As the bread was dished out, she only took one slice.

"I've had more to eat than you two already today, you need it more than me," she explained.

Abigail made a sandwich out of her food and bit into it. The loaf was dry but she was more than used to that by now. Although the fat was chewy, it was a fresh and tasty chewy that she hadn't experienced for a long time - if she closed her eyes it was just like having a beef sandwich back home, something that reminded her of their father. If their mother was ever out for the night, preparing the evening meal would be his responsibility. Cooking wasn't really his forte so dinner would always be a simple – but delicious – plate of fried steak, eggs, and mushrooms. If there were any leftover potatoes, Abigail would pester him into frying those up as well. As much as she enjoyed the splendid meals that her mother cooked, sometimes Abigail wanted nothing more than a hearty plate of junk food.

Once they had all finished eating, they sat there staring at the candle for a while. The stiffness was returning to Chana's hands and arms, and being on her feet all day was beginning to catch up with her. However, she was glad to be back with her family and she wanted to savour the moment for a little longer.

Abigail began blowing softly at the candle, watching in fascination as the shadows loomed and bounced around the room. The flame lurched and wobbled, reminding her of when she would spin around in the garden and try to walk in a straight line. She wondered why the flame always seemed so desperate to hang onto to its place at the top of the candle. Was it like an honourable soldier doing his best to stand to attention? Or was it more like a desperate prisoner who has been shackled to a post?

Leo pursed his lips together and blew the candle out. Abigail was startled by the sudden descent into darkness and she blinked her eyes rapidly as the night threatened to overwhelm her senses. For a split second it was as if she were standing on the edge of the world, staring down into the abyss.

"Oops," Leo said quietly. Although he couldn't see it, Abigail frowned at him.

"Boys," she muttered.

Chana felt a flush of annoyance run through her. With the candle no longer lit, there was little else to do but go to bed. She opened and closed her hands a few times, trying to work the stiffness loose. Hopefully they wouldn't be too sore tomorrow.

"I guess it's time to go to sleep," she sighed.

Leo remained still. He could tell that they were annoyed with him so he didn't want to be the first person to get up.

Abigail yawned. "Night, then."

She stood up and carefully made her way to the bedroom, holding her hand out to guide her in the darkness. Just as she began wondering if she was going in the right direction, one of her knuckles knocked against the doorway. She let out a sound of displeasure and threw a scowl in Leo's direction.

Within five minutes they were all drifting off to sleep.

***

## Chapter 5

Two days later Abigail woke up wondering what day of the week it was. Their clocks and watches had been sold and traded a long time ago, so keeping track of the time and the date was far harder than it used to be. The days themselves were long, arduous, and boring, whilst the scarcity of food meant that mealtimes were sporadic and inconsistent. More often than not, Abigail found herself not really caring whether it was morning or mid-afternoon. When your stomach is empty and you don't know if the next person to come through the door will be friend or foe, such things seemed unimportant.

She rolled over and looked across the room, keeping hold of the blankets so that they didn't fall onto the floor. Leo's bed was empty, so Abigail assumed that he was in the bathroom. She turned over onto her back and stared up at the ceiling. A cobweb lay in one corner looking discarded and forgotten about, causing Abigail to wonder where its owner had gone. Was he hiding in a tiny crack somewhere, or had he made another home elsewhere? Maybe it wasn't just people who went hungry in the ghetto.

As Abigail lay there, she became aware of how silent the apartment was. Leo wasn't the quietest of people even in his sleep, so she should have heard him moving around by now. She sat up on the edge of her bed and placed her feet on the floor. A small chill ran up her legs and she reached down for her shoes... only to discover that they were no longer there. A feeling of dismay and loss surged through her as she tried to figure out how her most precious belongings had disappeared in the night. She looked over at Leo's empty bed again and immediately became suspicious: surely it couldn't just be a coincidence that both her shoes and her brother were absent at the same time? Was it part of a mean boy's trick? Was he hiding them somewhere out of reach?

Abigail stood up and walked as far as the bedroom doorway, looking and listening for any sign that might tell her where her shoes were. A sudden faint sound from outside the apartment sent a rush of adrenaline and panic coursing through her, and her eyes bulged in their sockets as she caught sight of the doorknob slowly twisting itself open. Abigail wanted to turn and run away as fast as she could, not wanting to see the faces of the monsters who would sneak in to steal her shoes and her family as they slept. Terror consumed her as the door began opening inwards, the tiny squeak of hinges sounding loud and deadly. A head peered round, one that was as dirty and as grubby as any of the monsters that filled her nightmares, one that she recognised only too well. Just as the tendrils of a scream began to take hold somewhere in her belly, she realised that it wasn't a monster at all – it was Leo.

The door opened some more and he stepped cautiously into the apartment, almost as if he were trying to sneak in without being heard. His eyes locked onto Abigail and a knowing grin appeared on his face, one that suggested he had been caught doing something he shouldn't be doing.

Leo came inside and closed the door behind him, not bothering to be quiet any more. He stepped forward and brought his hand out from behind his back, placing a package on the table. It landed with a familiar *clunk* that made Abigail's mind do somersaults.

"Happy birthday, Abbie," Leo said. "I was hoping for it to be a surprise and I'm not sure if they're dry yet." He gestured to the paper package with his hand and an embarrassed smile took hold on his face.

Abigail's mouth dropped open in shock. Was it *really* her birthday? She hadn't even thought about birthdays for a long time - after all, how could they possibly exist in this place of misery and suffering? Well, if someone has bought her a birthday present then it must be her birthday. And if it was her birthday, that means she must be... ten. Ten years old today. Ten, ten, ten.

She let the number bounce around in her head a few times, trying to get a feel for it. She wasn't eight, she wasn't nine, she was *ten*, a big number to be proud of. It was double figures and it felt strange to finally get to this point in her life. She had always assumed it to be an age that lay off somewhere in the distant future, one that always seemed unattainable. It was an age that she had considered to be the point whereby she would be big and strong, and no-one would be pushing her over or saying mean things about her.

Abigail stepped towards the table and carefully touched the bag. The soft crinkling sound reminded her of being at home and unwrapping her presents in the lounge. For a fleeting moment she thought that Leo was going to impatiently tell her to hurry up and open it as he always did. She turned the bag round and slowly tore it open. Her mouth dropped open in amazement, and she blinked a few times as she tried to make sense of what she was seeing.

*Birthday shoes! I've got new birthday shoes!*

The shoes were immaculate and beautiful, shiny and wholesome and real... or so she initially thought. A tiny bolt of disappointment ran through her when she saw that they were actually her old shoes. She picked one up and examined it closely: the heel had been replaced and there was some new stitching down the side. They felt newer and sturdier than they did the night before, and they had been polished and buffed to perfection.

"Why don't you try them on?" Leo suggested. There was a hint of impatience in his voice.

Abigail set the shoes down on the floor and stepped into them. When she flexed her toes the shiny surface seemed to pulse and glow up at her.

"Just like new," Leo said.

Abigail looked up at him, her eyes brimming with happiness. "No," she disagreed. "They *are* new. These are my brand new birthday shoes."

She stepped forward and hugged Leo as hard as she could. An idea popped into her head and she took hold of his hand. There were smudges of what looked like dried shoe polish on his fingers.

"Dance with me. I want to dance in my new shoes," she told him.

Leo wasn't much of a dancer and he agreed only with some reluctance. There were a few awkward moments when neither of them was sure who should be leading, but they just about managed to work out some kind of rhythm. Leo did his best not to step on her toes, whilst Abigail giggled whenever he bumped into one of the chairs. Leo gazed into his sister's eyes, feeling himself being drawn into the warm and happy world that she always seemed to live in. He wanted to know what her secret was, wanted to know how she managed to keep her spirit alive all the time. They danced and twirled around the table a couple of times and then stopped and smiled at each other. Abigail opened her mouth to say something, when a loud sound startled her. The two of them looked around and saw their mother standing in the bedroom doorway clapping her hands.

"You two looked adorable!" Chana announced. "What a sight to wake up to!"

Abigail did a perfect little curtsy and Leo performed an awkward bow, causing their mother burst out laughing.

There were a few other, simpler presents for the birthday girl. She was given a colourful marble, an empty cigarette packet to go with the others she already had, a toy train that was small enough to fit inside a Christmas cracker, and a bar of chocolate. Abigail insisted on sharing the chocolate out, although she saved herself some for later.

Once the celebrations were over, they made their way to the soup kitchen for some breakfast. Chana recognised one of the ladies serving the food out and she made a point of introducing her children.

Abigail did her best to make sure that no-one stepped on her new shoes - when she sat down, she tucked her feet back under her chair so that they were kept well away from everyone else's dirty toes.

After they had finished eating they went back to the apartment. Chana had a nap before setting off for work, whilst Leo announced that he had some things to do and disappeared not long afterwards. Abigail let out a big sigh. It was now the third day in a row where she was being left alone up here in this boring place. She stood up and walked over to the window, hoping that something interesting might be happening outside. Over on a roof she spotted what looked to be a cat lying down on its side. She kept her eye on it for a solid minute or so but it didn't move at all. Although a small voice in the back of her mind was telling her that it was probably dead, Abigail decided that it was just sleeping.

A smile spread across her face when she saw the man on the bicycle go past. The usual questions of who he was and where he was going filled her head, and she wanted to open the window and call after him. Abigail leaned forward and let her head rest against the glass. Her breath began fogging the window up and she slid her nose around to draw little shapes in the mist. Something caught her eye and she saw that a small column of smoke was rising up from the bombed out building again. Once more, her mind was filled with curiosity and questions about what was going on over there. She cast a glance towards the door, wondering whether she should go out or not. Although it could be dangerous outside, she didn't think she could take another day of being stuck in on her own and if she kept to the quiet areas she should be okay. After all, she was ten now and everyone knows that ten is more grown up than nine.

Abigail walked across the room, her footsteps sounding loud and heavy on the bare wooden floor. She pulled open the door and stood there for a moment, staring down into the abyss. The steps looked cold and unyielding, whilst the apartment behind her suddenly seemed warm and inviting. A small gasp escaped from her mouth when something moved down at the bottom of the stairs, something small and brown. She tentatively went down a few steps, doing her best to be silent. When it moved again she could see that it had a tail, and a happy thrill ran through her when she realised what it was: *a mouse!* Before she could move any closer, the mouse disappeared into the hole near the bottom of the stairs. Abigail rushed down and tried to peer inside it, giggling excitedly the whole time. She couldn't *wait* to tell Leo that she had been right about it all along and that he didn't always know the answer to everything.

After waiting patiently for another minute, she stood up and realised that it wasn't going to be coming out again anytime soon. However, the fact that she had seen the mouse meant that her decision to leave the apartment was entirely justified, and the outside world didn't seem quite as threatening as it did before. Abigail stepped out onto the street and closed the door behind her. The first thing she noticed was the row of holes on the building on the opposite side of the road, and she decided to go and take a look at them. Now that she was up close, she wondered if it was possible for a bullet to go all the way through a brick wall. It reminded her of the time spent in the garden back home, wondering how deep all the wormholes and ant holes went.

When she ran her fingers round the outside of the holes, specks of brick dust crumbled beneath her hands. She slid a finger slowly inside as far as she could, wondering what she might find. Something felt loose at the back of the hole and a small object fell out when she snatched her hand back. She bent down and picked up what seemed to be a flattened lump of metal, turning it over in her hands. Was this what happened to a bullet when it hit a wall? It was fascinating to see something as feared and as deadly as a bullet reduced to nothing. She twirled her finger around in the other holes as well, but found nothing in them other than grains of dirt. As she slipped the bullet fragment into her pocket, she spotted what looked to be a young boy playing with something in the gutter. She looked around for any adults but couldn't see anyone who might be looking after him. Abigail began walking towards the boy, who didn't look up as she approached, and it wasn't until she was only a few feet away that she realised he was playing with a dead pigeon.

"Hello," Abigail said in a friendly voice.

The child looked round and smiled at her. "Birdy go fly!" he announced in a cheery voice.

Abigail blinked. She was horrified at the thought of letting him play with a dead and dirty animal, but it would break her heart to tell him that it was dead.

"Where's your mummy?" she asked.

"Mummy is gone," he replied. A deep frown appeared on his face that was almost comical. "Mummy is gone!" he repeated, speaking as if it was Abigail's fault.

"Oh, I'm sorry," she said, feeling mortified. "Here, would you like some chocolate?" she asked, fumbling around in her pocket.

The boy looked at her in wonder. "Choc-choc?" he asked, not quite believing it.

Abigail broke a small piece off and handed it to him. The sheer delight on his little face filled her with happiness.

"You be my mummy?" he asked through a mouthful of brown mess.

"Of course I'll be your mummy," she smiled.

In a way she felt flattered that he had asked that question and she couldn't stop herself from ginning at him. He grinned back at her and they giggled happily at each other.

"What's your name?" she asked.

"Ham," he answered proudly.

Abigail frowned, not sure if she heard him correctly. "Ham?"

Ham nodded enthusiastically.

"Where do you live?"

The boy thought for a moment. "In orphage," he told her, stumbling over the word.

It took Abigail a few moments to understand what he meant. "You mean the orphanage?"

"Orpharage," Ham confirmed.

A wave of pity washed over Abigail. It seemed that Ham had no family and no-one to look after him. She wondered how he even ended up here in the street all by himself, and started wondering what she was going to do with him. The apartment was just round the corner, but what would mum and Leo say? What would they feed him with?

She sat down on the curb next to Ham, doing her best to shove the dead pigeon away whilst he was distracted.

"Birdy no fly?" he asked.

Abigail shook her head and gave him another small piece of chocolate. He grinned at her again, causing his entire face to light up. It was a sight that she didn't think she would ever get bored of, and she tenderly stroked his cheek.

*Halt!*

Abigail snapped her head round, suddenly aware that something was wrong. Whoever it was that had just shouted at them, there was a strange aggressiveness in their voice and a feeling of horror trickled down her spine as the blocks of understanding began falling into place.

The road was on a slight hill and a soldier was standing at the top, silhouetted against the dull grey sky. Abigail noticed that he was holding a bottle of some kind and he threw his head back to swig from it. He wiped a hand across his mouth and took an unsteady step forward.

*Halt!*

The soldier staggered sideways as he shouted and had to use his arm to stop himself from falling against the building beside him.

"Silly man!" Ham said, clapping his hands.

Abigail looked down at him and shook her head. What was she going to do now? The soldier seemed to be drunk - was that a good thing or a bad thing? Her only real experience with drunk adults was of her father sitting outside in the garden with a bottle of wine. Although she didn't like the way it made his voice sound so strange, the silly things he said and did were always funny. Sometimes he would even give her piggy backs and pretend that he was going to tip her into the pond.

"Come on, we've got to go," Abigail instructed Ham. She did her best to sound less frightened than she actually was.

She grabbed his hand and started running down the road, but after only a few steps she could tell that he wasn't going to be able to move fast enough.

*Halt!*

She glanced back over her shoulder and a fresh wave of panic washed over her as the soldier fumbled for something on his belt. Abigail reached down and picked Ham up so she could carry him. There was an alleyway not too far away and she began stumbling her way desperately towards it.

"Mummy, trousers falling down," Ham complained right next to her ear.

Abigail carried on running and tried to readjust her hold on him. The alley didn't seem to be getting any closer, yet Ham was somehow getting heavier and heavier with every passing moment. She battled to keep control of herself, desperate to avoid falling over and bursting into tears. Why hadn't she stayed inside? Who cares if she saw a mouse, who cares if there is smoke coming from a building, who cares if she is ten? Why isn't Leo here? Leo was always there when she needed help, always there with the right answers to everything, always there when -

The sound of a gun being fired echoed and bounced its way down the street, causing Abigail to flinch and stumble. Ham was slipping through her arms again and she was vaguely aware of the sound of breaking glass, a noise that seemed to go on forever. The entrance to the alley was there, right there, yet she *still* hadn't managed to reach it and the soldier was going to be bearing down on them at any moment, ready to beat them with his strong fists and his terrible weapons.

*Halt!*

As she approached the turning Abigail swore that she was gradually moving slower and slower... yet somehow she finally reached it, somehow she had made it around the corner, somehow she had put a solid brick wall in between them and the soldier. Ham suddenly slipped through her exhausted arms and he let out a confused cry as he tried to keep his balance.

"Why Mummy cross?" he asked.

Abigail ignored him and glanced around, looking for somewhere to hide. She spotted an overflowing dustbin in a doorway and dragged Ham behind it.

"Mummy needs you to be quiet," she whispered, putting a finger over her lips.

Ham nodded, his eyes wide and staring.

The sound of heavy footsteps filled the air, footsteps that were being made by someone in big, heavy boots that could crush and maim anyone who got in their way. They became louder and louder until Abigail was sure that the soldier was standing right on top of them. Tears began streaming down her cheeks and she readied her hand so that she could clamp it over Ham's mouth if he started crying. When he looked at her, his face was pale and clammy with fear. Abigail wanted nothing more than to hold him, to show him how to make animals from bits of paper, to feed him chocolate, and to be his mummy. Instead, they were in this dreadful place hiding behind a bin that stank of rotten meat and faeces *and it wasn't fair.*

She could hear the heavy breathing of the soldier, causing her to clamp her eyes shut in the hope that he would just go away. How many seconds was it going to be before he tossed the bin aside and found them? What terrible things was he going to do to them? Why were there so many mean people who wanted to hurt her?

The soldier cursed and threw his bottle onto the floor, sending brown shards of glass scattering in all directions. Abigail flinched so hard that it was almost a convulsion and Ham's bottom lip began trembling. She shook her head and tried to mouth the word 'No' at him, but she could barely even control herself now. Her vision was a blur and the entire world was nothing more than a wobbling, quivering mass. She placed her hand over Ham's mouth, hating herself for it. When he began to struggle she had to fumble her other hand round the back of his head to keep him still. She felt his tiny hands latch onto her arms and grip her tightly. Was he holding onto her for comfort, or because he was scared and

66

he wanted her to let go? She was trying to be his mummy, yet right at this minute she felt more like a bully.

There was the sound of a man cursing, followed by heavy footsteps stomping away from them and Abigail whimpered with relief. She remained still until the footsteps had disappeared completely, not quite able to believe that the soldier hadn't found them. As she slowly removed her hands from Ham's face, his whole face started to twitch. Abigail felt something rising up inside her and this time she decided to just let everything go. The two of them just looked at each other for a moment, before Abigail pulled him towards her and hugged him as hard as she could. Although she started crying before he did, Ham soon caught up and for a short while it was just the two of them in their own little world where there was no ghetto, no soldiers, and the rotten stench of the dustbin had been blown away.

As Abigail hugged and rocked Ham against her chest, a sense of realisation slowly dawned on her: of all the times that she had been reduced to crying away in a corner, this was the first time she hadn't had to do it alone.

***

# Chapter 6

Although Chana was getting used to her journey to the soup kitchen, she still felt uncomfortable being outside all on her own. Every so often she would glance up at a window and catch sight of a forlorn figure staring down at her. They were always pale and gaunt with sunken eyes, and she began to wonder if she was being stalked by ghosts. Somewhere in the back of her mind, there was the niggling worry that some of those people were actually reporting on her - after all, who could tell what was happening inside all these buildings? Was there an extensive network of note-takers and informers, waiting for the chance to denounce people to the Germans? How many hotlines had been set up for this purpose?

*You say there is lone Jewess walking down Nalewki street? This is good information and we reward you with half a loaf of bread. If she is pretty Jewess, we no wipe bread on our arses first. If you lie to us, we punish with hammers. If we think you lie to us, we punish with hammers. If we run out of bread, then too bad for you!*

Chana quickened her pace and was relieved when she arrived at the entrance. There was the usual unsettling sound of a gigantic chain being dragged across something large and metallic, before she was finally making her way down the stairs. As she walked into the main kitchen area a small frown appeared on her face. Kasia and two of the other women were standing together in a tight circle, speaking in hushed tones. She wondered what nonsense they might be gossiping about.

"Hello," Chana said, announcing her arrival.

Three heads snapped round and looked at her, revealing pale faces with grave expressions plastered across them. There was a moment of silence, almost as if the entire world had decided it didn't want to speak.

"What's the matter?" Chana enquired.

"There's going to be another shipment soon," Kasia ominously remarked.

Chana frowned again, sensing that they weren't telling her something. "Oh, that's good," she began. "We haven't had any meat for a couple of days now. Even if it's just fat rinds, at least it's something extra to put in the stew."

Kasia took a deep breath. "No, not that type of shipment. I mean there's going to be a shipment out."

Chana blinked and said nothing. That peculiar feeling of being out of sync with the rest of the world came creeping back - it was as if they were talking to her in code and she was using an outdated translation book.

One of the women put a hand up to her mouth. "Chana... haven't you heard about what's being going on?"

Chana shrugged in confusion. The way they were looking at her now, she wondered if someone was trying to creep up on her from behind.

"Do you know about Treblinka?" Kasia asked.

Chana shook her head.

The women looked at each other. "It's a camp that the Germans have been sending people to," one of them said.

"What, like a work camp?"

"No," Kasia replied. Her voice cracked as she spoke. "People get sent there and are never seen again."

A cold chill ran up Chana's spine. "What do you mean? Who gets sent there and where do they go?"

"It's a death camp. The Germans round people up and load them onto a train. The train goes to Treblinka... and the people are murdered when they get there."

Chana suddenly felt sick and lightheaded. A thousand questions filled her mind, yet she found herself unable to utter so much as a single word. Her mouth opened and hung there uselessly, almost as if the rest of her face had decided to cast it off like a reject. She felt like an actress at the theatre who has not only forgotten her lines, but also who she is and why she is standing there dressed as a tree. Every time she tried to make sense of what she was being told, her mind did another somersault. It was as if someone was repeatedly pulling the rug out from under her, continually sending her spinning out of control. For a brief moment her grip on reality began to slide away, sending her down the slippery slopes of insanity.

Chana reached out, looking for a chair. Some hands grabbed hold of her and guided her down. When she rested an arm on the table, she wondered why it felt so soft and squashy; she had flattened someone's bit of cake.

As the initial shock wore off, all of her questions began to untangle themselves. Why was this happening? How had it started? Who had made the decision to start killing innocent people for no reason? Who was driving the trains? Who was laying the tracks? Who was doing the murdering and how were they describing their job role to their friends and family? How would you even apply for such a job in the first place?

Finally, Chana was able to speak. "How many are being killed?" she croaked.

"Lots," came the frustratingly vague answer.

"What, like hundreds?"

"We hear different things from different people. Some of them witnessed it themselves and were able to escape," explained Kasia.

"How many?" Chana persisted.

"We've heard that Treblinka isn't the only camp that the Germans have built. Thousands of people are being sent to these places every week from all over Europe."

Chana felt her grip on reality loosening again. Whenever she read an article in a newspaper about unsolved murders, she could understand how the killers were able to go about their grisly business undetected - it was one person acting alone and it required nothing more complicated than a sharp kitchen knife. However, to kill so many thousands of people would require a huge operation involving an immense number of willing co-conspirators. How was it possible to get something like that started? What about all the other people who were indirectly involved? What about the engineers and the architects who built the camps? What about the plumbers and the electricians? Did they know what was being done once their work was completed? Were they telling anyone about it? How was it possible for such a thing to happen and for no-one to do anything about it? She thought back to the other day when the fairground music had been playing on the other side of the wall - was it really that easy to ignore these crimes of humanity when it was happening to someone else?

Chana managed to get control of herself again and saw that the others were now seated as well. They remained in silence for a few moments.

"What're the Jewish Council doing about it?" asked Chana.

"There's nothing that they can really do. They're almost as powerless as we are," Kasia lamented.

There was another period of silence. Chana realised that she was chewing at her nails, something that she hadn't done since she left school. When she pulled her hand away from her mouth, her teeth loudly snapped shut. She decided that she didn't want to talk about death camps any more.

"Have we got any meat for today?" she asked.

"Actually, we have," one of the ladies said. She seemed relieved that they were talking about something else. "It looks a bit stringy, but it's better than nothing."

Five minutes later, they were hauling out sacks of vegetables and getting on with their work.

*** 

As they approached the orphanage, Abigail could see that it was a bigger building than she had realised. Although it looked quite large from a distance, it seemed to have swollen in size during their journey. She looked down at Ham and wondered how his little legs were doing. Although she had carried him part of the way, his constant wriggling made her arms ache.

"Mummy coming in orpharage?" he asked.

Abigail wasn't really sure how to answer this question. Although she would very much like to go in with him, it wasn't really up to her. Up close the orphanage itself was big and daunting - in her mind she had always imagined it to be a happy place of balloons and rainbows. She adjusted her grip on Ham's hand, realising that this might be the last she saw of him. If nothing else, Abigail hoped that he would remember her - she certainly wasn't going to forget about him.

They walked slowly towards the main entrance door and Abigail swallowed hard as the building filled her vision entirely. She knocked on the door and waited patiently for someone to answer it. Ham made a cute little noise with his mouth that at any other time would have made Abigail laugh. There was a loud click that made her heart beat a little faster, and the door opened to reveal a man standing behind it. Abigail suddenly realised that she had no idea what to say. What if Ham wasn't actually from the orphanage at all? He was only four years old, so he might have just repeated something he heard from someone else. What if this man accused her of stealing him? And why was a man here? She had expected it to be a lady answering the door.

"Hello," the man greeted her in a pleasant voice. "Can I help?"

"Erm, yes. I found this boy in the street and he said he was from here. Do you know him?" Abigail replied. She was starting to feel a bit stupid. Even if Ham *was* from here, how on earth was this man - who was no doubt just a worker or a cleaner or something - going to recognise him? Most kids looked alike, and this bald man with a beard and glasses probably had no idea -

"Ham? Where did you get to? You really need to stop wandering off like that," the man scolded.

Ham giggled and buried his face against Abigail's leg. This exchange took Abigail by surprise and she didn't know what to say.

"Sorry, allow me to introduce myself," the man said to her. "My name is Janusz Korczak and I run the orphanage here. Ham is known for his disappearing acts, he's quite the little explorer!"

Ham laughed again and Abigail got the sinking feeling that the conversation was coming to an end. In a few moments, this man was going to take Ham back and then close the door on her. She would never, ever see him again.

"What's your name by the way?" Janusz asked her.

A ray of hope popped into her mind. Surely he would only be asking this if he was genuinely interested. "Abigail. My name's Abigail. Abigail Nussbaum. Sir," she blurted out, trying to remember how adults greeted each other in times like this. She even offered her hand out for him to shake it and to her utmost surprise he smiled and accepted it.

"Pleased to meet you, Abigail. Thank you for bringing Ham back here safely, I dread to think what might have happened otherwise."

A horrible feeling ran through her when Ham went over to Janusz. Her hand suddenly felt cold and empty, and she looked at it in surprise. She looked down at Ham again, knowing that these were their last few moments together... unless, of course, she took some drastic action.

"Can I come and work here?" Abigail blurted out. "I mean, not to get paid or anything. But to help out. I really like children and I can show them things and play with them and just help out. If you'll let me of course." The effort left her feeling breathless and as vulnerable as she had ever felt. Her legs felt like jelly and if he told her to go away she wasn't sure if she would be able to stop herself from bursting into tears.

A frown of consideration appeared on Janusz's face and there was a moment of silence. "How old are you, Abigail?" he enquired.

"I'm nine," she replied eagerly. With a panic she acknowledged her mistake and immediately realised that she had blown her chances already. "No, I meant I'm ten! I'm ten, really I am! I'm ten!" She stood up on her tiptoes, as if to accentuate just how ten she was.

Ham giggled, thinking that this was some kind of game. "Mummy coming in, too?" he asked, reaching up towards Abigail.

Janusz let out a chuckle. "Well, I guess it would be rude not to invite her in for a while. Come on in, Abigail. If Ham trusts you, then so do I."

Joy and relief swept right through Abigail as she could scarcely believe that she was being invited inside. She followed them into a side room where about twenty children of various ages were sitting in clustered groups, whilst three nurses in blue and white uniforms kept an eye on them.

"Abigail, I'll leave you with Ham and his friends for now. If you need help with anything, feel free to ask me or the nurses. I'll let them know you're staying for a while."

Abigail smiled and nodded. Now that she was here, she felt as if she were being pressured into things - playing with children was more fun when you didn't have people watching over you.

"Hello," she said to a small group sitting on the floor. "I'm Abigail."

Two of the kids looked up at her and waved.

"She my mummy!" Ham proudly announced.

All four of them stopped what they were doing and looked up at her curiously. There was an element of awe on their faces.

"Mummy want to play?" one of them asked, holding up a yellow wooden block.

"I'd love to play," Abigail replied, crouching down next to him. "Shall we build a house? One that we can all live in and have fun together?"

The children clapped and laughed eagerly. There were only ten blocks or so, but Abigail handed them out one at a time and told them where to place it. What they ended up with was more of a rounded pen than a house, but by then their imaginations were in full flow. Abigail tore up some small strips of paper and gave one to each boy, before placing her own strip in the middle of the blocks.

"See, now that's where Mummy will sleep. Show me where you're going sleep," she told them.

"Me sleep next to Mummy," Ham said, placing his bit of paper next to Abigail's.

"Can I sleep next to Mummy?" one of them asked.

"You can all sleep next to Mummy if you want," she told them. They all duly put their bits of paper next to Abigail's.

She reached into her pocket and took out the small train that she had received earlier. "Look at this. If we want to come to the orphanage, we can go by train," she said and started pushing it along the floor. "Choo choo! Choo choo!"

The children let out squeals of delight and clapped at her. Abigail couldn't help but laugh with them, and she glowed with pride. Her earlier nerves were banished entirely and it was almost as if she were back in the local synagogue. Their faces were now all looking at her expectantly as she grabbed a piece of paper from one of the tables.

"Look, watch this. See this bit of paper? I'll show you some *magic!*" Abigail told them.

She started folding it this way and that, talking to them as she did so to keep their attention. They sat in rapt silence as the paper seemed to shrink before their very eyes.

A minute later, she held it up her hands. "Ta-da!" she announced. "Look, it's a bird." She tugged at the tail and the wings flapped up and down slightly, sending the boys into squeals of delight again.

"Birdy go fly!" Ham loudly announced.

Abigail handed the bird to him and grabbed another piece of paper. Within another couple of minutes she had produced a dog that could bob its head up and down. The first bird that she made was slowly being taken apart, so she quickly created another one for them to play with. When Abigail looked around she realised that her audience had grown considerably - at least half the kids in the room were looking over at what was going on, as were all the nurses. She set about making a few more shapes for them, including a tree that could stand up on its own and the kids laughed and giggled when she cocked the dog to one side and pretended that it was urinating up against the trunk.

For the next hour, Abigail coached the nurses and some of the older children on how to make the simpler shapes. Some of them eventually got bored and went back to what they had been doing before but one or two stayed behind for a while longer. Abigail noticed that one older boy in particular kept looking over at her and it began to make her feel nervous. He was bigger and stronger than she was which was usually bad news.

"Um, hello. You're Abigail, right?" he asked.

"Yes," she replied in a small voice.

"Ah, good. That's, er, a really nice name," he complimented.

Abigail looked him, not quite believing what he had just said. She couldn't remember the last time a boy had said something nice to her. It took her moment to respond but she managed to squeak out something that sounded like a thank you.

"My name's Antoni by the way," he told her.

Abigail nodded at him but remained silent. When he took a casual step towards her, she glanced nervously away.

"How old are you?" Antoni enquired.

"I'm ten," she replied, feeling a bit bolder. There was no way someone in an orphanage could be *that* old.

"Oh, okay," he replied. "I'm eleven."

Abigail's heart sank. He was bigger, stronger, and older than her. She edged slightly away from him, bracing herself for when he tried to push her over.

"But ten's a good age," he added. "I remember I felt all grown up when I first turned ten. Really, it's just the same though."

Abigail looked at him again. There was no aggression in his voice and she couldn't see anything threatening about his body language. She also noticed that instead of his hands being clenched into fists, he was rubbing his palms together. At first she thought he might be cold, but she slowly realised that he seemed nervous or maybe even a bit shy. But what did he have to be nervous about? He was big and strong; possibly even the oldest boy in the room.

"Those shapes are really good," he persisted.

"Thank you," she replied.

A smile appeared on her face, an involuntary one that took her by surprise, but when Antoni smiled back at her she looked down at the table again. Out the corner of her eye she could see that he was still staring at her. Abigail dared a glance back at him and was astonished when he smiled at her once more. Her cheeks turned bright red and she felt herself blushing without really knowing why. A warmth spread through her that initially had her worried, until she realised that it was a nice, pleasant feeling.

"So, er, how did you learn to make them?" Antoni asked.

Abigail just stared at him for a moment, only now noticing that his hair was a bright red colour. She remembered that the handful of children in her school who had red hair were bullied mercilessly by the same boys who pushed her over. She also noticed that his face was clean, far cleaner than most of the people she saw walking around in the ghetto. Abigail presumed that there were baths and maybe even soap here in the orphanage.

"Was it something the teachers showed you at school?"

Abigail blinked herself back to reality. For reasons she couldn't explain, she felt flustered and confused. "Erm, yes. Well, no. I found a book in the school library and sort of practised them whenever I could."

"Wow, you must be really smart," he told her, sounding impressed.

Abigail let out a small giggle. It was a reaction that confused her, as no-one had said anything funny or amusing. Before she could say anything else, the sound of a ringing bell filled the air.

"Oh, it's time to go and eat," Antoni said. "Are you eating with us?"

"Erm, I don't know," Abigail admitted.

One of the nurses came over to them. "Abigail, you can go in with them if you want. You've certainly earned it."

As they walked towards the door, Antoni bent down and picked something up off the floor. "Here, don't forget this," he said, putting something into her hand.

It was the toy train she had brought with her and she slipped it back into her pocket, wondering how she had forgotten about it so easily. Abigail followed Antoni and the other children into a large room that was full of tables and chairs. The younger ones sat down and waited as the nurses brought plates of food to them, whilst the older ones stood in a queue to get theirs.

Abigail spotted Janusz standing over on the other side of the room. He waved to her and she waved back.

"Janusz is really nice," Antoni told her. "He knows everyone's name. He's like a dad. At least, I think he is."

It took Abigail a few moments to realise what Antoni was saying. "Haven't you ever had a dad? I mean, ever?"

"No," he confessed. "Both my parents died when I was young,"

By now they had reached the front of the queue, and Abigail watched in wonder as a generous serving of mashed potato was dropped onto her plate. A beef sausage somehow appeared right next to it and a splash of gravy materialised out of thin air. She followed Antoni to a table and sat in the seat just opposite him. The cutlery had already been laid out and Abigail wondered if she had been sent to a holiday camp. This was a proper meal that she could eat with a knife and fork, and if the spoon was anything to go by there was going to be a dessert as well. There was a brief moment where she worried that this might all be part of an elaborate German trick. She poked at the sausage with her fork, half expecting it to burst like a balloon. As she cut a small piece off and placed it into her mouth, she was reminded of her father's fried meals.

"So who are you here with?" Antoni asked.

Abigail blinked herself out of her daze. "Mum and Leo," she told him. "Leo's my brother. My dad died after we came here."

"Oh, that's sad. What did he die of?"

Abigail thought for a moment. "I don't know," she answered truthfully. "No-one could do anything for him. He started getting headaches and it wasn't long before he was spending nearly all day in bed. He was barely eating anything and then one day he just..." she let the sentence trail off and looked down at her plate. This was the first time she had ever talked to anyone about how her father died, and she was surprised that she was willing to say so much to someone she had only just met. Maybe it was the fact that he was being nice to her, or maybe it was because he had never known either of his parents. Even though she had watched her father slowly wither away and die, she still had a family whilst he had nothing.

Abigail glanced around the room, realising that there looked to be about a hundred or so children in here now. Some were as young as three or four, whilst one or two looked as if they might even be older than Antoni was. She began to wonder what everyone's story was, and how many of them had ever known their parents. Was it possible that there were sets of brothers and sisters in here?

When she turned back around, Abigail saw that Antoni was staring at her again. She held his gaze for moment before blushing and giggling without knowing why. They resumed their meals and talked about their respective lives in the ghetto. When Antoni said that he spent most of his time in the orphanage and rarely ventured out, Abigail was surprised at how similar their lives seemed to be. There was brief lull in the conversation and Antoni let out a large belch. Abigail looked at him in shock for a moment, unable to believe that he had done something so rude and disgusting.

"Sorry, I'd completely forgotten that... oh no, I'm really sorry," Antoni said, his face turning red with embarrassment.

Just as she was considering how to tell him off, Abigail surprised herself by bursting into laughter. She had no idea why it was so funny - maybe it was way it had suddenly come out of nowhere, or maybe it was the childish way in which he had looked so utterly ashamed of himself - but the more he tried to apologise, the more she laughed at him. Once their laughter had died down, they noticed that dessert was being served and as they rejoined the queue, Abigail spotted Ham over on one of the tables. He looked over and waved eagerly at her, his bottom lip smeared with food. She waved back at him.

"You seem really good with the kids," Antoni told her.

"Really? I just like having fun with them," she replied.

"Yeah, you are. You also seem more grown up than others of our age."

"What do you mean?" Abigail asked, not sure if this was a compliment.

"I dunno, really. Just the way you speak, and even the way you hold your knife and fork at the table. It's good, I quite like it."

A feeling of pride swelled up inside Abigail. She didn't really know what to say, so just mumbled a thank you. When they reached the front of the queue again, a slice of cake was dropped into a bowl and handed to them. As she carried it back over to the table, Abigail stared at it with something akin to wonder.

Once the meal was finished, both Antoni and Abigail went back to the same room that they had been in before. They played with Ham and the younger children for a while, until Janusz approached them.

"Abigail? It's going to be getting dark soon," he told her. "You should probably get going before then."

A deflating sense of disappointment settled on her; she had forgotten all about going home.

"Don't worry, I'll let you say goodbye first," Janusz said, smiling.

Abigail stood up and went over to Ham. "Ham? I've got to go home now."

He reached up towards her. "Mummy give me hug bye?"

When she picked him up he leaned forward and gave her a big kiss on the cheek. Abigail kissed him on the forehead and stroked the side of his face. It was tender and soft, something that seemed completely out of place in the ghetto. She was filled with a desire to take him with her, slip out past all the guards and the soldiers, and take him somewhere safe.

"Is tickles!" he giggled.

She reluctantly put him back down and ruffled his hair. Out the corner of her eye she could see that Antoni was watching her again. Although she wanted to say goodbye to him as well, she felt strangely nervous about it. How did a girl say goodbye to an older boy?

She turned and faced him. "Goodbye, Antoni. It was nice to meet you,"

"Yeah, it was nice to meet you too, Abigail."

He held his hand out and she took it. His hand closed firmly around hers and for a moment she thought that he was going to crush her fingers. A tingling sensation ran up her arm, and she wondered if they were ever going to see each other again.

Janusz showed her out. "Abigail, it's been wonderful having you here. Earlier, you asked about coming here to help out. Are you still interested in doing that?"

Abigail's eyes lit up. "Really? You mean that?" she asked.

Janusz smiled. "Of course! The children really like you, and those paper shapes you made were marvellous. The nurses have been full of praise about you as well."

Abigail blushed red. "Okay, sure, I'd love to. I'll try and come back tomorrow if that's okay."

"Please do! And then the day after that as well! Any time after ten in the morning is good, as everyone will have had breakfast by then."

Abigail said her goodbyes and headed off back to the apartment. Initially she was in such high spirits that she forgot where she was and it wasn't until a German truck almost ran her over that she snapped out of her daydream. When she arrived back at the apartment, Leo was there waiting for her.

"Where'd you go?" he asked. There was a sternness to his voice.

"I got a job at the orphanage," she replied.

Leo raised his eyebrows. "What? Seriously?"

Abigail told him about the boy she had found in the street and how she had taken him back to the orphanage, but skipped the part about having to run away from the soldier.

Leo's face softened.  "Okay, fair enough.  A lot of people would have just left him in the street.  You probably saved his life."

This shocked Abigail.  The thought of little Ham being left at the mercy of the ghetto was too horrible to imagine.

"The man who runs it is really nice," she said, preferring to talk about the pleasant side of things.

"Janusz?  Yeah, he adores those kids."

"You know him?" she asked, sounding surprised.

"Sort of.  I've never spoken to him, but I know he's a very brave man.  The orphanage used to be on the other side of the city before the Germans came.  Janusz was given the choice of escaping the ghetto, but he didn't want to abandon all those children."

"Really?" Abigail asked.  "So why didn't they let them stay where they were?  Why did they all have to come in here?"

Leo shrugged.  "Why did any of us have to come here?"

Abigail opened her mouth and then shut it again.

"The Germans are monsters, Abbie.  Monsters doing terrible things to people."

"Like what?" she asked in a small voice.

Leo looked at her for a few moments and let out a long sigh.  How much was he supposed to tell her, and how would she react?  Was it fair to tell her?  She could be randomly yanked off the street tomorrow - didn't she have a right to know why?

"They send people to places that they never come back from.  Big places, out in the countryside.  No-one ever sees them again."

Abigail felt as if she was back in nursery again, being told a fairytale about ogres who steal children and take them back to their caves.

"Do they... die?" she asked.

Leo chose his answer carefully.  "Only the ones that don't manage to escape," he said, hating himself for it.  It was about as cowardly an answer as it was possible to give and he felt like a politician trying to squirm his way through an awkward interview.

A chill ran down Abigail's spine.  There were questions popping up in her head that she didn't really want answers to, yet she felt powerless to stop asking them.  "Could it happen to us?"

Leo's jaw flexed and his lips pressed themselves together. He reached out and took one of Abigail's hands, marvelling once again at how clean she always seemed to be. Earlier this morning he had been dancing with her, yet now he was breaking the news that some men she had never met before were plotting and conspiring to murder her. He stroked her hand and thought back to when she had been born.

When his sister first came into the world, Leo was a mere seven years old. She had been born prematurely, so his first glimpse of her had been from behind a thick glass wall. He remembered seeing his mother lying in the hospital bed looking tired and dishevelled, a sight that had unsettled him. The doctors decided that his mother and his sister should remain at the hospital for a couple of weeks, a decision that didn't sit right with his young mind. Her absence made the house seem empty, and he noticed that mealtimes were far less interesting than they used to be - if it wasn't a plate of fried beef and tomatoes, it was likely to be cheese on toast and half a tin of peaches for afters.

Leo had never forgotten the actual day that Abigail was brought into the house. He had been standing at the top of the stairs when his mother - who for some reason now looked very different - walked in through the front door, carrying a basket under her arm. Inside the basket was a strange pile of white sheets and as he peered over the banister, Leo thought he caught a glimpse of something small and pink.

"Leo," his father had said to him. "Come and say hello to your sister."

He traipsed nervously down the stairs and into the front room where his parents had disappeared to. His mother came over and kissed him on the head, thanking him for being such a good boy. He didn't actually know what she was talking about but he wasn't one to argue when he was being complimented. Now that he was standing in front of her, he could see what was different about his mother: she was much thinner, and her swollen belly had shrunk.

His parents told him to sit on the chair, and for a moment he thought that they were going to tell him off for not tidying his room. Instead, his mother reached down into the basket and pulled out a small white bundle, before placing it carefully in his arms.

82

"Leo," she said in a soft voice. "This is Abigail, your new sister."

He looked down at what had been handed to him, feeling somewhat confused. Was this *really* his sister? All the other sisters he had ever seen were tall girls who played hopscotch and talked about silly things that didn't matter. From what he could see, Abigail was nothing more than a scrunched up face in a bundle of white cloth. The only thing that suggested it was actually a girl, was a small pink bobble that had been stitched to the blanket. All those months of waiting and watching as his mother struggled with the physical burden... what was it for? It all seemed like such an anti-climax.

As Leo sat there wondering what he was supposed to be doing, something happened that caused him to let out a small gasp. At first he thought it was just his imagination, but Abigail's eyes had started to open. Although it wasn't much more than a slit, he could just about make out the tiny glimmer of her eyes. They gradually opened up some more, and Leo found himself utterly captivated by the way she seemed to be looking directly up at him. Her mouth also opened, revealing the tiniest tongue he had ever seen. She shifted slightly in his hands and Leo felt what could only be tiny arms and legs moving around underneath the blankets. All of a sudden he realised that this delicate little bundle really was a person, that it would one day grow up to play hopscotch in the playground, that it was his sister, that it was a *she*.

When he looked up at his mother, a realisation had hit him. He finally understood where his sister had come from and why his mother was so much thinner than she had been before. He now understood that he had once been as small as this, that his mother had once carried him around in the exact same way that he had watched her carry Abigail around. Leo looked back down at his sister and gasped when he saw that her eyes were still wide open and focused intently on him. There was a beauty in her eyes that sent a rush of emotion through him, one that made him realise that all the struggles of the last few months really were worth it. Abigail's mouth suddenly opened again and she emitted a small noise that startled him.

When his mother moved in to put her back into the basket, Leo tensed his arms for a moment. He didn't want anyone to take her away, and he missed the soft warmth that had been filling his hands.

"She's amazing," he said.

"Yes, she is," agreed his mother. "You were amazing when you were born as well."

He had smiled at her then, surprised at how happy those words made him feel.

In the days that followed Leo was constantly at the side of Abigail's cot, hoping to be there at the exact moment she opened her eyes so he could experience that special moment with her again. As the months and years went by, he found himself sharing plenty of other moments with her: the first time that she coiled her entire hand around one of his fingers; the first time that she was sick on him; the first time she said his name; the first time she wobbled across the room to give him a soggy, half-eaten biscuit; the first time they got a phone line installed and she sat on the stairs all day hoping that somebody - anybody - would ring them; the first time when somebody *did* ring them and she didn't know what to do.

Each of these moments served to remind him of that very first time he saw her open her eyes, when he saw how beautiful and delicate she was. From that moment on, he vowed to do his best to look after her and protect her as best as he could.

"Abbie," Leo told her as they sat facing each other in the dreary ghetto apartment. "I'm doing everything I can to keep us safe from the Germans." He patted the top of her hand twice and slowly released it.

Abigail looked at her brother. Although she knew that he would do his best to look after her, she didn't see how he would be able to protect them from the full might of the German soldiers. She thought back to when the notice had first appeared in the local newspaper telling them that all the Jewish families were going to be moved to the Polish capital. At first she thought that it would be an exciting trip for them, as she had only ever been to Warsaw twice before. They had travelled by train each time and she had sat looking out the window, marvelling at how fast the countryside flashed by them. She loved the city itself too, and watching so many people walking around had filled her with a sense of wonder.

The noise, the smell, the coffee shops, the cars... all of it made her wonder why everyone was so unhappy about being moved there.

A few days later, German soldiers started appearing in their town. At first there was just the occasional military car driving along the roads, or pairs of soldiers sitting outside cafes. As the days wore on, more soldiers began to arrive and Abigail saw them doing mean things to people. An old man had a loaf of bread knocked out of his hands, whilst a woman pushing a pram was forced out into the road because none of the soldiers wanted to move out of her way. When the day of the move finally arrived, there was a sudden loud banging on the door that shook the entire house. It was as if an entire herd of horses had gathered outside and were taking it in turns to kick at the walls.

"Jews? Out!" a voice bellowed through the letterbox.

They had only been allowed to take a certain amount of their belongings with them, and there was a cart that they began loading their things onto. One of the German soldiers began to get impatient with how long they were taking and he barked at them to hurry up.

"Come on, come on! The rats don't take this long in the sewer when someone flushes the toilet! What're you waiting for?"

Leo had glared at him and replied with something in Hebrew, which took Abigail by surprise. She had never heard him speak the language before, and he had always been dismissive about Jewish customs and celebrations - on the rare occasions he bothered attending the local synagogue, he spent most of the time yawning and rolling his eyes.

Abigail watched the soldier's face turn red with rage and he stomped towards Leo, grabbing him by the shoulder.

"What did you say to me, you Jewish swine?" he bellowed. "What did you say?"

Abigail was shocked at how easy it was for the soldier to shake her brother around. Leo was the biggest and strongest person she knew and had always been the one who protected her. She had cried out, suddenly realising why no-one wanted to go this new place in Warsaw. She was fearful for the future; fearful for what was lying in wait for them. For the first time in her life, the spectre of anti-Semitism had come out from behind the shadows and bared its teeth at her. The soldier flung Leo to the ground as easily as if he were made of paper and Abigail covered her eyes. She felt someone rush past her and there was the sound of a familiar voice. As she lowered her hands, she caught sight of the soldier bring his baton down onto her father's head and the blow sent him sprawling on top of Leo.

*No!*

She had screamed at the top of her voice and burst into tears.

Once they finally got their few precious belongings packed onto the cart, they began making their way down the street. As they went past another house, Abigail saw that some German soldiers were nailing planks of wood across the front door. A distressed woman was shouting down at them from one of the top windows.

"Hey!" the woman cried. "My father is ill, we need more time to get him ready."

Abigail was confused about why the soldiers were ignoring her. She wanted to run up and shake them and say that the woman was there, right there, can you not see? If they would just wait a bit longer then everything would be fine.

As they went further down the road a soldier shouted something that confused her.

"Hey, little Jew. Where did your daddy hide all the money and the jewels? Was it behind the walls? Did he bake them into loaves of bread so that you could eat it all up?"

Abigail had no idea what the soldier was talking about, but his mocking tone upset her. She also noticed that Leo was keeping his head down and staying silent. At one point Abigail looked up and spotted a column of smoke rising on the horizon. It struck her as being an odd time of day for a bonfire as most people would be at work or school. As they rounded a corner, Abigail's eyes widened when she saw that someone's house was on fire. There were soldiers standing around outside the house, all of them pointing and laughing. A scream rang out and Abigail saw two crying women standing in the middle of the road. No-one did anything to help them.

The further down the road they walked, the longer the procession of carts grew and people were coming out of their houses to watch them go. Most of them stood and stared, whilst others shouted and jeered. Abigail wondered why these people were saying such terrible things to her. There was nothing that she had done to them, nothing that could possibly make them hate her so much. Someone threw a stone that hit their cart and made a loud *crack!* sound. It had only missed Abigail by a few inches and she cried out in surprise. The cart was all that they had left in the world, and for a split second she thought the entire thing was going to fall apart. Leo shouted something and the stone thrower disappeared back into his house.

Abigail had tried retreating into her own world for a while but nothing seemed to work. The road was nothing other than an uncompromising sea of grey and she was too on edge, too frightened that someone would sneak up behind her and push her over. After a while she burst into tears again and it wasn't long before she felt strong hands reaching for her, strong hands that could pick her up and dash her against the ground if they wanted to. A familiar voice told her that everything was going to be fine, that everything was going to be okay once the war was over. She had believed him then, she had no reason not to. Whenever Leo told her that things were going to be okay, they usually were.

As Abigail sat there in the apartment listening to Leo tell her that he was doing everything he could to keep them safe, she wondered if she still believed him. His face was firm and there was a defiance in his eyes that she had seen many times before.

"Is the war going to be over soon?" she asked him.

Leo raised his eyebrows at this question. There seemed to be several wars going on at the moment, so the answer would depend on which one she was referring to. He decided not to bore her with too many details.

"Things are going badly for the Germans in the east," he told her. "The Russians are counter-attacking and fighting like beasts."

Although this was true, Leo knew that it was a double-edged sword. As things got worse for the Germans, so too would things get worse for anyone inside the ghetto. A bully likes to pick on the weaker targets and right now the Nazis were the biggest bullies of them all. If the losses continued to stack up on the battlefield, the Germans would begin diverting more and more resources towards exterminating those who were powerless to resist. Why bother building tanks when you can make plans for genocide instead? Why would any self-respecting Nazi officer want to go anywhere near the bloodbath that is the Eastern Front? Getting permission to build another death camp is a far more enticing prospect. He would have his own office, a nice house on the premises, and a steady supply of slave labour to polish his shoes. He could even take his children on a visit to the kennels and let them pet the guard dogs.

"The Russians? Are they on our side?" Abigail asked. There was scepticism in her voice.

Leo reached out for his sister's hand again. He rested the tips of her fingers on his palm and casually spread them out. When he squeezed them back together, he made an explosion noise with his mouth.

Abigail let out a small giggle. "What're you doing?" she asked.

Leo shrugged and laughed. "You always seem so clean. I might wait until you're asleep and smear mud on you."

It took her a heartbeat to realise that he was only joking, but by then she had already snatched her hand back.

"Don't you dare!" she exclaimed, trying to hide her smile.

Leo screwed his face up and twisted his hands around as if he was impersonating the Hunchback of Notre-Dame.

"I'm going to cover you in poo and make you stink forever!" he said in an eerie voice.

Abigail made a small squealing noise, and Leo chased her round the table. With every step he made a fart noise, and she giggled as if she didn't have a care in the world. He quickened his pace and was able to reach out and grab her, pulling her towards him.

"I'm going to eat you and then spit you out again, and you'll be all covered in goo!" he said in the eerie voice.

"No, not that!" she giggled, playing her part as the captured princess.

"You two look like you're having fun," said a voice.

Leo and Abigail both looked up and saw their mother standing in the doorway. Neither of them had heard her coming up the stairs.

"Yeah, Abbie was bullying me again," claimed Leo.

Abigail made a face at him. "Boys," she muttered.

Chana smiled at them, although it was a weak one. Leo now noticed how dark the room had become: the night had crept up on them without them noticing and in the gloom he thought he saw tension on his mother's face. Although she looked tired, there was something else as well.

"I managed to bring us some food again," Chana told them.

She placed a bundle on the table and inside was some cake and a loaf of bread. After the discussions about Treblinka, none of the ladies had felt like eating very much so there was quite a bit leftover.

"Wow," said Leo. "All I managed to get was this." He opened one of the cupboards and took out a tin that had no label. "I'm not sure what's in it, though."

Abigail lit a candle and carefully placed it in the middle of the table. Leo got the tin opener and grunted as he strained to prise the lid off of the can. He peered inside and saw what seemed to be a shifting mass of flesh - it was only when put it under his nose that he realised it was a tin of cherries.

Abigail told her mother about the visit to the orphanage. She included the parts about the meal and the paper shapes, but once again left out the bit with the German soldier.

"Antoni lost both his parents when he was a baby," she told them.

There was a pause.

"Who's Antoni?" Leo asked.

Abigail looked at him quickly. "He's, erm, one of the boys at the orphanage."

"Oh, right. How old is he?"

"Eleven," she replied in a small voice. She shot Leo an awkward sideways glance and felt herself blush for reasons she still didn't quite understand.

Even in the candlelight Leo saw her face change colour. He laughed and took hold of her hand for the third time that evening.

"Good for you, Abbie. Good for you," he told her.

After they had finished eating, Abigail disappeared into the toilet. Chana leaned in towards her son and spoke in a hushed tone.

"Have you heard about..." she began. She paused, realising how stupid the question might sound. "Do you know what Treblinka is?"

Leo's face turned serious. "Yes, I've known about it for a while," he admitted.

"Does Abbie know?"

Leo shrugged and made a see-saw motion with his hand. "Not exactly. I told her a few things but nothing specific."

Chana nodded. Her face looked grim. "What're we going to do?" she asked.

"Things are being sorted out, we'll be okay."

Chana opened her mouth but the flush of the toilet interrupted her. She leaned back in her seat just as Abigail emerged from the bathroom.

"I'm going to go to bed," announced their mother. "Today has been tough."

Leo and Abigail followed her lead, and once the candle was blown out the apartment was immediately plunged into a sudden, paralysing darkness. Abigail carefully walked into the bedroom, sat down on her bed and flexed her toes. Although she couldn't see them, she knew that her new birthday shoes were gleaming back up at her. As far as she was concerned, they were as fresh and as dainty as when she first got them. She eased them off her feet and gently slid them under her bed.

As she lay there drifting off to sleep, Abigail thought about the fun she had had at the orphanage today. She remembered Ham's happy smile and the excited cries of all the other children. She also remembered Antoni, though she couldn't place the actual reason why. For what seemed to be the first time in her life, Abigail found herself looking forward to tomorrow.

***

# Chapter 7

Abigail knocked on the door of the orphanage and waited patiently for someone to answer. She noted how strange it was that on the other side of this door lay what seemed to be a paradise of happiness, innocence, and joy. There was a small click and the door began to open. A moment of doubt and nervousness consumed Abigail as she wondered if they really wanted her to come back again. What if the invitation had only been made out of politeness? How many children were going to go hungry because she was being given a meal?

"Ah, Abigail! Welcome back! We've been expecting you, please come on in," Janusz told her.

Abigail smiled in relief and stepped inside.

"My dear girl, it seems that word of your talents have spread right through this place," Janusz said. There was a twinkle in his eye that reminded Abigail of a cheery uncle. "I'd like to introduce you to some other children, if that's okay?"

"Sure, that'd be great," she replied, smiling bashfully.

Janusz led her into a side room that looked a bit bigger than the one she had been in the day before, although the interior was largely the same. Three nurses in white uniforms were keeping an eye on about thirty children who were sitting in different groups. One child in particular looked up as she entered the room and his face lit up.

"Mummy!" cried the boy.

He ran over to Abigail and stretched his arms eagerly up at her. She paused for a moment, not sure if she should be picking up him up or not. A maternal instinct kicked in, overriding her nervousness and she hoisted him up into her arms. He planted a wet kiss on her cheek and beamed at her.

"Little Ham has been asking after you all morning actually," Janusz said with a chuckle.

Abigail smiled with happiness and found herself unable to stop looking at Ham's cheeky grin. He held up a crumpled, misshapen bit of paper.

"Birdy no fly," he said in a sad voice.

Abigail laughed and put him down again. She took the bit of paper and wondered how many hands it had passed through to get in such a state, whilst Ham watched in wonder as she carefully unfolded and repaired the bird. A minute later she handed it back him.

Ham looked at it curiously for a moment. "Birdy go fly?" he asked.

Abigail reached down and tugged at the tail. Although the wings didn't flap as smoothly as they would on a freshly made bird, it was enough to make Ham squeal with delight.

"Abigail, you've worked your magic again!" laughed Janusz. "It seems you don't need me anymore, so I'll leave you to it."

Abigail let Ham lead her over to some other children that he had been playing with. He grabbed a piece of paper from one of the tables and handed it to her.

"You do doggy?"

Abigail sat down and made sure that she had the attention of the children around her. They all watched in curiosity as her hands expertly flipped the paper over and over, slowly turning it into something recognisable. Once it was finished she walked it across the floor and made a barking noise. The children all laughed and clapped, with Ham doing his best to be the loudest out of all them.

As the rest of the morning wore on, Abigail's audience gradually swelled in size. The nurses remained at the back of the crowd, happy to just watch this curious young girl as she effortlessly entertained so many children at once. Shortly before lunch a shadow loomed in the corner of Abigail's eye.

"Hello," said a large boy.

Abigail looked around and saw Antoni standing next to her. He seemed slightly nervous, almost as if he wasn't sure if he was allowed to be there.

"Hello, Antoni," replied Abigail. She felt an odd sensation in her stomach that was close to sickness, although she was sure that she wasn't ill. Was this what the adults meant when they talked about getting butterflies in your belly?

A look of relief settled on his face the moment she said his name, almost as if he had been worried that she wouldn't remember who he was. "We'll be eating soon," he said. "We can go and sit at the table again if you like."

The sound of a bell rang out and everyone in the room moved towards the door.

"Sure, that'd be great," Abigail replied. She smiled at him and he smiled back.

Lunch itself was a simple cheese sandwich with some slices of apple, but to Abigail it was almost like eating a luxurious feast. She wondered how it was possible for the orphanage to get all this food. Did the Germans allow more rations in for the children? If so, why? It didn't seem to make any sense - there were thousands of other children who needed food in the ghetto. She thought back to what Leo had said about Janusz, about how brave he was. Although he seemed to be a very nice man, he didn't seem to fit into what she thought a brave person would look like. Maybe he had managed to work out some kind of deal with the Germans. After seeing the things that they were capable of doing, she realised that maybe he really was as brave as her brother had said he was.

"We can go and sit in the garden if you want," Antoni suggested.

"Garden? Really? There's a garden here?" she asked, wondering if there was no end to the joys and miracles of this place.

Antoni didn't say anything in reply, he just nodded as if she had asked him about the existence of the sky.

They went out through a door at the rear of the building, whereby Abigail saw that the 'garden' was nothing more than an open concrete area. A few other children were out here, along with a nurse who was sitting on a wall and keeping an eye on them. There was a faint unpleasant smell in the air that caused Abigail to wrinkle her nose up and it took her a few moments to realise that it was just the usual stench of the ghetto.

Over on the far side of the garden was a trapdoor with a sign above it saying *Waste Here*. Abigail stared at the two words, picturing them in her mind to try and decipher exactly what they were telling her. The whole ghetto was full of people wasting away - perhaps that was where they all ended up. If she opened up the trapdoor would she find Mr Karski somewhere below?

Wild weeds were sprouting up through the ground and Abigail bent down to pluck a long, thin leaf. She carefully rolled it up from one end to the other and twisted it between her fingers a few times.

"It's like a little telescope," she said, holding it up to her eye. "Maybe a mouse could use it to keep an eye out for the housecat."

Antoni laughed, and Abigail felt herself shrinking back inside her shell.

"No wonder the kids love you so much," he told her. "You see things that no-one else sees. It's as if you can create a dream world out of nothing."

Abigail looked at him, unsure if he was mocking her or not.

"You've got a fantastic imagination," he continued. "It's a special talent."

"Most people just make fun of me," Abigail confessed. She flushed red, scarcely believing that she had admitted this to someone.

Antoni shrugged. "So? Some people just can't deal with the things that they aren't the first to see. There were probably people who laughed at Leonardo da Vinci the first time he started playing around with his paints."

Abigail looked at him, feeling something akin to shock. She wanted to say something but her throat felt as if it was made of stone.

"No-one's ever said anything like that before," she managed to croak.

Antoni shrugged again. "No-one like you has ever been to the orphanage before."

Abigail had no idea how to respond to something like that so she just remained silent. Antoni was worried that he had made a fool of himself so he too decided not to say anything for a while.

The next two weeks provided Abigail with some of the most enjoyable moments of her life so far. She went to the orphanage every single day and loved every minute of her time there. However, it was also a rather confusing time for her as she was exposed to feelings and emotions that she hadn't ever experienced before. Ham was always delighted to see her, and the sight of his cheery smile never failed to send a surge of maternal love running through her. She found herself wanting to spend the entire day hugging and holding him in her arms, just so she could stroke his face and listen to him laugh with his friends.

There was also the enigma that was the boy who called himself Antoni. Or rather, her feelings towards him were enigmatic. She enjoyed spending time with him and when she caught him looking at her in that strange way it sent a pleasant warmth running through her. Although he was bigger and stronger than her, it was almost as if he didn't realise it - at no point did he ever try to bully or intimidate her and instead of being scared by his size, she found it comforting. Sometimes she found herself gazing up at his bright red hair and wanting to reach out and touch it. Antoni also introduced her to some of the other older children, all of whom seemed pleased to meet her.

The nurses were polite and friendly towards her as well, always treating her as if she was an adult, whilst Janusz was patient and understanding to the point of being father-like. The young children looked up to her as if she was a loving mother, whilst the older kids treated her like a friend. She was getting two good meals a day at the orphanage and they even let her use the showers. The water was warm, there was soap for her to use, and the nurses sometimes even washed her clothes for her too. Abigail considered stealing a bar of soap to take back to the apartment but she simply couldn't bring herself to do it.

In some ways, Abigail felt like her life had returned to normal. In fact, it was as if her life had never been better.

*\*\**

It was a pleasant Tuesday morning and Abigail looked up at the sky. Although the sun was out and the clouds were nowhere to be seen, the air wasn't particularly warm - if you stood in the shadows it wouldn't be long before you were putting your hands in your pockets and hunching your shoulders against the chill. A crow flew overhead, cawing loudly as it went and Abigail wondered if it was in pain. When you can fly, at what point does the ghetto stop being the ghetto? How high would you have to go to escape the dead zone and be away from the suffering? The bird disappeared from view and Abigail let out a small sigh. They had just finished eating at the soup kitchen and her mother was talking to the man who guarded the door. Despite the fact that her mother worked there, Abigail had never seen the man smile at them. It was almost as if he resented not being able turn them away when it was busy.

Abigail's thoughts turned to the orphanage. It was still too early to go there just yet, but she was looking forward to being back inside what must be the safest place in the entire ghetto. She traced a finger round in a circle on her left palm and thought back to what had happened the day before. She had been sitting out in the garden with Antoni when she suddenly realised that they were holding hands. Although she struggled to remember exactly how it had happened, the intensity of that moment was still clear and fresh in her mind. An electric shock had run up through her arm and she kept looking down at their linked fingers just to make sure she wasn't imagining things. At first she had left her hand limp and uncommitted, thinking that maybe it was just a mistake, but when Abigail tightened her grip Antoni immediately did the same. His hand was large, strong, and warm, and her first thought was that he was going to snap her fingers as if they were twigs. Neither of them said anything or even dared to look at each other and they just sat there in silence for a while. It was only when Ham came rushing up to her that the spell was broken. When she picked him up he had given her one of his trademark sloppy kisses and babbled something about how he loved his mummy. Out the corner of her eye, Abigail could see that Antoni was looking at her in that funny way again. When he smiled at her, she thought how nice it would be if the three of them could go on a trip to the woods together.

"Abbie?" enquired a familiar voice. "Is that a smile I see on your face?"

Abigail was dragged back to the present and saw that Leo was looking at her with a roguish grin on his face. Her own face flushed red.

"I was..." she began, feeling flustered. "Just thinking about... things."

"Thinking about Antoni again?" persisted Leo. He winked at her and laughed as her face turned an even brighter shade of red. He stepped towards her and put an arm around her shoulders.

"Abbie, if you've found someone who makes you happy then that's great. If anyone deserves a bit of happiness, it's you," he told her.

Abigail let out a small chuckle and looked up at him. "Thanks, Leo."

He playfully pinched her nose. "And if he breaks your heart then I'll break his legs."

"You two ready to go back?" interrupted Chana.

Leo and Abigail nodded in unison, and the three of them began walking back in the direction of the apartment. A minute later they turned a corner and found themselves confronted with the peculiar sight of a long line of people standing in the middle of the road. Abigail frowned, noting that the line consisted entirely of children standing together in pairs. In fact, she thought she recognised one or two of them.

"Some of them are from the orphanage," she remarked. "They must be off on a trip somewhere."

The children were all dressed up in their smartest clothes and a man was walking amongst them, making sure that everyone was buttoned up and that all the boy's caps were set straight. The man was bald, wearing glasses, and looked very familiar.

"That's... Janusz," Abigail said to no-one in particular.

Abigail suddenly felt confused. The line was so long that she was unable see both ends, meaning that the entire orphanage must be going out on this trip... but a trip involving such a large number of children would require a considerable amount of planning and preparation - there was the transport to be arranged, lunches had to be made, and spare clothes taken along in case the youngest ones had an accident of some kind... all of which would take time to arrange and everyone would be talking about it. So why had no-one told her about it? She would have been more than happy to help out.

"Oh my God," someone cried out. Abigail thought it might have been her mother but couldn't say for sure.

"Those *monsters!*" wailed another voice.

Abigail wondered who they were talking about. Surely not the children? And surely they weren't talking about either Janusz or the nurses who worked so hard to look after the children each day. Maybe someone in the crowd was doing something mean, although Abigail couldn't see anything monstrous going on. As she thought about it some more, an unpleasant light turned on somewhere inside her mind.

"Where are they going?" she asked, looking up at her brother.

When Leo looked down at her, his face was pale and full of horror. "Abbie," he said, swallowing hard. "They're not coming back."

"What...?" she asked, looking back at the line.

Some of the youngest children were holding bits of folded paper in their hands and another unpleasant light turned on inside Abigail's head when the line started moving. The nurses busied themselves with making sure that everyone remained together in neat pairs, whilst someone in the crowd said a strange word that sounded a bit like *Treblinka*.

"No," Abigail croaked.

Her mind was beginning to unravel all the whispers and overheard conversations of the last few weeks. She thought back to what Leo had told her; about what she had heard her mother and brother talking about when they thought she wasn't paying attention; the snippets of gossip that people exchanged in the soup kitchen. A sudden bolt of understanding hit her and everything appeared all at once in her head.

*Everyone is crammed into large carriages as if they are nothing more than cattle. A single bucket in the corner serves as a toilet for more than fifty people and before long the contents are slopping out all over the floor. The journey lasts for more than a day and there isn't enough room for anyone to sit down.*

*When they arrive, they are unloaded and forced to stand in a long line. There are two gates, a left one and a right one, with a man telling them which one to go through. If they are sent right, they are put to work until they die of starvation, disease, or exposure. If they are sent left, they are shoved into a large underground chamber and told to take their clothes off. The door is slammed shut and sealed. Fifteen minutes later the door is opened up again and every single person who entered the chamber is now dead. The people who were sent through the gate on the right are ordered to check the bodies for jewellery on their fingers and gold fillings in the mouths. Once everything of value is extracted, the corpses are then tossed into ovens and fire pits.*

*Innocent men, women, and children are sent to their deaths en masse. Whole families are wiped out in a matter of minutes. Entire villages and communities are decimated. The Nazi death machine is ruthless and efficient, and no-one is spared.*

Abigail spotted a flash of bright red hair somewhere in the procession of children and a sudden rage ran through her, igniting a fury that she didn't even know existed.

"No, no, *NO!*" she screamed at the top of her voice.

Abigail spun around and slammed her fist into Leo's arm as hard as she could. "You said you were keeping us safe!" she screamed at him. "Why don't you do something?"

Leo stared down at her, unable to believe that any of this was happening. He felt utterly powerless and had nothing to say. His face was grey and pale, and his legs were little more than useless twigs that struggled to support him.

Abigail's eyes began to burn as hot tears poured down her face. She turned back around and watched helplessly as over a hundred children walked passively and willingly to their deaths. Although she wanted to go and say goodbye to every single one of them, her body remained rooted to the spot. Everything that she considered precious was being torn apart and she could do nothing but watch it happen. She covered her face with her hands and wept uncontrollably. She thought of kind, brave Janusz; she thought of dear, happy Ham; she thought of Antoni and how happy he made her feel; she remembered them as friends, as children, as family, and as loved ones. Abigail removed her hands and looked up so that she could see them all one last time... but the street was empty and the people of the orphanage were gone forever. All that remained of her world was dust and memories.

A strong hand clamped down hard onto her shoulder and pulled her to one side. She felt herself being crushed up against someone big and strong, someone that could snap her in half if he wanted to.

Abigail closed her eyes and the world turned black.

\*\*\*

Leo lay his sister down on her bed and carefully took off her shoes. They looked as spotless and as clean as the day he had given them to her, and he placed them under her bed where he knew that she liked to keep them. He pulled the blankets up and stood there looking at her for a while. She always slept so soundlessly and still that sometimes he wondered if she was actually hibernating.

Leo's bed groaned as he lowered himself onto it and he let out a long sigh. He felt angry and ashamed - angry at the Germans for what they had done; ashamed at himself and everyone else for just standing there and letting it happen.

Although Abigail was sleeping peacefully now, he was worried about what was going to happen when she woke up. Leo had noticed how much happier his sister had been since she started working at the orphanage. Was this going to be the thing that finally broke her spirit once and for all? He lay back on his bed and closed his eyes. There were plenty of things that had almost broken his own spirit, starting with the initial German invasion of Poland. Although the politics of it all bored him to tears, he had contemplated signing up for the army when war had first been declared. It hadn't taken long for his parents to talk him out of it, but it wasn't something that he had seriously considered doing - it was mostly an empty gesture of defiance at his father's plans for Leo to take over the family business, something that Leo had no interest in doing. He despised the jealous hording of wealth that every business owner indulged themselves in, counting every penny as if it were something that they could take with them when they died. As far as Leo was concerned, it was no coincidence that the most influential people in the local Jewish community were also the richest. Money and faith were constant sources of tension between him and his father. Leo didn't want anything to do with either, whilst his father coveted both.

When the notices about the ghetto first started appearing in all the newspapers, Leo had been incensed. Herding so many people into such a small area was an outrage, yet their Jewish leaders stood back and did nothing. What was happening to the mountains of cash that they all boasted about? Why wasn't it being used to barricade and fortify the roads?

It wasn't until the day of their eviction that the realities of the Polish surrender began to sink in. In amongst the sea of German soldiers was a startling number of local police constables, all of them wearing the same sneering and hateful expressions that the Nazis exhibited so well. To be invaded and conquered in a matter of weeks was humiliating enough, but having to watch your fellow countrymen cosy up with the enemy and prise you out of your home as if you were nothing more than an annoying limpet on the side of a ship... it was soul destroying.

And of course there was the death of his father. Yes, they had had their disagreements. No, they didn't really see eye to eye on many things. But family was family and Leo was protective of them. Watching his father turn from a proud man who provided his family with whatever they needed, into an ashen-faced bed-ridden vegetable was devastating. No-one could do anything for them, not even to tell them what was wrong. Leo was certain that it was caused by the soldier who had hit him over the head that day, but even that was nothing more than an uneducated guess. When his father had finally passed away they realised that they had no idea what to do with his body. Eventually they managed to get in touch with some people who gave a short sermon in the apartment before taking him away on a cart. Leo's last memory of his father was watching as he was rolled up into a grubby white sheet. The body was taken downstairs and loaded up onto a wagon where two other bodies in sheets already lay. As they shifted the corpses around to make room, an arm slid out and hung down the side of cart. Leo was nearly sick.

In the days and weeks afterwards, Leo had roamed around the ghetto looking for solace. He didn't really know what he wanted, but he knew that he needed something. He needed answers, he needed friends, and he wanted revenge.

And that was how he met the blonde girl with the red cap.

***

# Chapter 8

The girl with blonde hair looked down at her feet and wiggled her toes. Although her shoes were made of thick, hardy leather there was just enough movement to let her know that her toes were all present and accounted for. She pulled a cap from out of her coat pocket and eased it onto her head. The mirror in her room was cracked and broken, meaning she had to duck her head down to check that the cap was on straight. She considered something for a moment and pulled out a small black cylinder from her other pocket. When she twisted the bottom, a small stub of lipstick popped up out of the darkness. The girl applied it sparingly and delicately, all the while reflecting at how absurd something like vanity seemed here in the ghetto. There were people out there begging for the smallest scraps of food, yet here she was trying to make herself look pretty. She certainly wasn't the only woman to bother with such things; far from it in fact. Down at the marketplace there were females of all ages handing over absurd sums of money for tiny morsels of cosmetics.

Alenka pursed and stretched her lips, watching her reflection in the mirror. On the surface of it, worrying about her appearance seemed irrational and senseless, yet in some ways it was more important than it had ever been. Every time that bright red nub of lipstick twisted its way towards her, a small part of normality returned to her life. It was a sensation that lasted for no more than a fleeting instant, but it was a powerful and irresistible one. Sometimes it was so strong that she felt as if she could reach out and grab it, yet it would be gone before she could even blink. There were times when she would repeatedly twist and untwist it, desperate to recreate that sensation, but it was impossible to do so on a whim - it was as if it were a supernatural power that could only be used sparingly and the compulsion made her feel like an anxious clock-watcher who couldn't resist glancing up at the time every few minutes.

Vanity also stopped her doing other things that would be practical to do here in the ghetto. For instance, she could quite easily borrow - or steal - a pair of scissors and cut all her hair off. It would mean she wouldn't have to worry about it getting dirty and tangled, whilst the problem of lice would go away in an instant. Yet why *should* she do these things? The Germans had already taken away her home, her friends, and her family. They had starved her and made her live in squalor, and tried to rob her of her dignity. But the one thing they couldn't take from her was the fact that she was a woman, and if preserving that meant she would occasionally have to go hungry then it was a price she was willing to pay.

Alenka had a meeting to go to and she didn't like to be late. She glanced instinctively down at her wrist, looking for the watch that was no longer there and the empty spot on her arm sent a pang of sadness through her. Giving up the watch had broken her heart, but she knew that a beggar can't afford the luxury of being a chooser.

These days the entire concept of timekeeping felt like a German psychological trick that they used to keep their prisoners in check. She glanced out the window but the clouds blocked her view of the sun. Although the height and position of the sun wouldn't actually mean anything to her, it was nice to at least have the option of being able to rationalise a random guess of what the time might be.

Alenka made a final readjustment of her cap and felt under her blouse to make sure her Star of David necklace was still around her neck. It was only a cheap, flimsy thing but it was important to her. She sighed and decided to head out for the meeting. If she was early it might mean she would be offered an extra cup of tea. If she was late then it was just tough luck and she would have to drink faster. After picking up the tube of lipstick, she shoved a small wedge of cork into the open end. The proper lid had been lost long ago so she had to make do with what she had.

When she stepped out into the street, Alenka slid her hands into the pockets of her jacket. Although her shoes were heavy and practical rather than small and dainty, they were still quieter than any of the high-heeled shoes she had worn. She actually preferred walking boots over anything else - they lasted longer and she wouldn't have to go home to get changed if she was sent off on a long errand somewhere. They were also good for kicking things, something that had saved her skin on more than one occasion in the past. Like many of the other Jewish girls she knew, Alenka had learned how to fight at an early age and the faint scar on her arm served as a reminder that long nails can be just as lethal as a fist.

Over on the other side of the road stood two German soldiers, both of them wearing sullen expressions of arrogance. Alenka wondered if either of them actually knew what he was doing here in the ghetto. Did they see themselves as guardsmen? If so, what exactly did they think they were guarding? Other than despair, filth, and dilapidated buildings there was nothing for them to be in charge of. Or maybe the soldiers saw themselves as moral guardians of the peace - whilst their fellow soldiers waged death and destruction in other parts of the world, there they stood making sure the Jews of Poland didn't get too rowdy.

Alenka snatched the cap off of her head and stuffed it back into her pocket. Although it was dark red in colour, sometimes she worried that it drew unwanted attention to her. The desire to blend into the crowd was made all the more complicated by the fact that she had long blonde hair. There were times when she would put the cap on to hide her bright locks, only to take it off an hour later when she thought people were staring at her red hat.

She came to a door and knocked on it twice. There was the clunking sound of a sliding bolt being released and the door opened a few inches, revealing an inquisitive face. Alenka nodded once and was beckoned inside.

"Go on in," the man told her. "Stefan's waiting for you."

She nodded a second time and went through a door on the right. The room was pleasantly decorated whilst a warm fire gave it a homely feel. A man in his late twenties was sitting cross-legged in a chair reading a book.

"Ah, Alenka," he greeted her. "Please, sit down."

Alenka sat down. The chair was comfy and she could have quite happily remained in it all day. Stefan poured some tea out for both of them. Although the crockery was plain and simple it made a pleasant change from drinking out of empty tin cans, whilst the crack that ran down the side of the teapot lent a kind of rustic charm to the proceedings.

"How's things?" Stefan enquired.

Alenka shrugged. "I'm still alive. No-one's tried to shoot me yet."

Stefan nodded. "It must be that red hat of yours, it makes you practically invisible."

There was silence for a moment and Alenka became aware of the faint *tick-tock* of a clock somewhere in the room. A smile appeared on Stefan's face and the two of them began to chuckle at a private joke.

"The Germans are stepping things up a gear," Stefan told her once they had settled down. "We're going to need to get a move on."

"What have the Jewish Council said about it? Are we going to get any help from them?"

Stefan scoffed. "No, they're a bunch of old men who are blind to whatever is put in front of them. No matter how many witnesses I drag in with me or how many reports I shove under their noses, they simply refuse to see the threat to us."

Alenka rolled her eyes in frustration.

"Quite," Stefan quipped. "Yet again, they've voted against taking any kind of armed resistance. We can't wait any longer if we're going to do this."

"So we're on our own then?"

"Not entirely. I've managed to make contact with another Polish underground group and they've agreed to a meeting."

Stefan leaned forward and topped their cups up. Someone came in and placed a small plate of sandwiches on the table, which Alenka eagerly tucked into. The bread was dry but she barely noticed.

"I'm sending you out to meet with them," he told her.

She nodded slowly. "Just me?"

"Yes. You have... certain persuasive charms and you can think on your feet. The meeting is taking place tomorrow afternoon out in the woods. There's a log cabin on the edge of a clearing and they'll be expecting you. You'll need to go down through the Muranowski tunnel and we've arranged for a car to drive you most of the way there."

Alenka sat there taking it all in. Although she had made use of the tunnel to run various errands in the past, this was a big step up from what she was used to.

"It's probably best if you go through the tunnel today," Stefan continued. "It'll make things easier on the other side."

This part of the plan was to Alenka's liking. It would mean she could sleep in a half-decent bed, get something half-decent to eat, and maybe even have a hot bath.

"What do you need me to say at this meeting?" she asked.

"Well, we still need more weapons and ammunition. We've already got pistols, grenades, and the occasional rifle. But it's not enough. Find out what they can supply us with and what sort of price they want."

"What're we going to pay them with?"

"Plenty of rich old Jews here in the ghetto still," Stefan replied, with a wry smile. "I'm sure if we rattle their mattresses and biscuit tins hard enough we'll hear the rustle of bank notes. There's also a trickle of funds coming in from outside groups and our friends in Israel."

Alenka said nothing and reached forward to take the last sandwich. They finished off the tea and made conversation for another twenty minutes until Stefan stood up, signalling the end of the meeting.

"Go on over to the other side as soon as you can," he reminded her.

Alenka left the house and put her cap back on - if nothing else, it would help to keep her head warm. Although she wanted to go over to the Aryan side straight away, she decided to mingle in the busy marketplace area for a while first. The likelihood that anyone was following her was slim, but it didn't hurt to take simple precautions. She stopped at the occasional stall and loitered in with the crowds of potential buyers. An old man with most of his teeth missing was looking forlornly at a set of dentures. Alenka thought about telling him that they wouldn't be of any use to him but decided against it - he probably didn't even have the means to pay for them and no doubt came to this stall every day just to stare.

Although the prices that people were being charged were high and outrageous, Alenka couldn't find it within herself to be too angry with the merchants. The harsh conditions of the ghetto meant that people were reduced to doing whatever was necessary to survive. Some people begged, some people stole, and some people set up businesses. Quite a few of those businesses were profitable, making their owners richer than they had ever been before the Germans came along. In fact, some of those businesses were downright exploitative and Alenka knew of at least one ghetto workshop that was busy recycling batteries for the Nazis. The owner of the workshop would pay a pittance to his employees who would have to hammer open old tank batteries and recover the reusable components. Gloves were too expensive for most of the workers, so it wouldn't be long before the poisonous chemicals caused their hands to develop painful sores that bled constantly.

Did this sort of thing bother Alenka? Not particularly. Life was complicated and no matter how unsavoury some of them could be, the world needed entrepreneurs. If there weren't any rich people here in the ghetto, how else was Stefan going to pay for the weapons that he was trying to stockpile? Of course, some of the less noble merchants had no problem with maintaining the status quo - after all, if the Germans went away the workshop owner had no-one to sell the recycled batteries to. In cases like this, Stefan would have to rely on threats of violence in order to get these people to open up their wallets.

"Hey, pretty girl," a stall owner called out. "I have something you might like."

Alenka stopped and looked down at what the man was holding.

"Fresh perfume that's not been touched!" he boasted.

Alenka picked up the small bottle and gave it a quick looking over. It was grubby, half-empty, and the contents were no doubt watered down to point of being worthless. She put the bottle down and decided that she had spent enough time getting lost in the crowds. The merchant yelled after her, but she ignored him.

When Alenka arrived at Muranowski Square she removed her cap and knocked on a blue door. A few moments later the door was answered and a man escorted her down into a cellar at the rear of the building. A single light bulb hung down from the ceiling but it did a poor job of illuminating their surroundings. The two of them slid a bookcase over to one side, revealing a concealed hatch in the floor. Alenka pulled it open and stared down into the narrow passageway underneath it. A short, sawn-off ladder was propped up against one side.

"Hope you don't have claustrophobia," the man remarked.

Alenka smiled grimly at him. "Want me to bring you anything nice back?"

"A postcard of the Taj Mahal would be nice."

She sat down on the edge of the opening and slowly lowered herself down into the hole.

"I'll see what I can do," she replied.

The hatch creaked as it was closed on top of her and she carefully shifted onto her hands and knees. The tunnel itself was cramped and treacherous, making it easy for unwary travellers to bang their head or an elbow, whilst the rounded sides made it look as if a giant worm were slowly working its way through the earth. A thin electrical wire ran along the wall and a solitary light bulb was all that existed to illuminate the first half of the tunnel. Blankets had been laid down to protect knees and hands but they tended to get dragged along and bunched up.

After shuffling slowly along for what seemed like an eternity, Alenka stopped for a brief rest. The light bulb shone brightly in her face and she had to close her eyes to stop herself from being blinded. Despite how cool and dry it was down in the tunnel she was beginning to perspire already, and the only sound she could hear was the rasping coming from her own mouth. She set off again and was quickly plunged into darkness as she inched past the light bulb. There was a sharp bend to the left coming up and she periodically held her hand out to find it.

Although she hadn't been directly involved with the construction of the tunnel, Alenka was more than familiar with its creation. It had initially started out as a tool of defiance against the Germans, a mere project for bored and angry ghetto inhabitants to channel their frustrations into. There hadn't been any real plans for it, other than using it as a means of escape. However, as time went on and as they began to realise the sheer scale of their task, the discussions about the tunnel's potential began to be discussed more earnestly. Their hopes had taken a nasty knock when they discovered that a large sewer pipe lay in their path, and it took three days of tears, teeth gnashing, and heated arguments for them to decide how to dig their way around it. But dig around it they did and the tunnel was eventually finished, allowing countless amounts of food, supplies, and weapons to pass through it each week.

A block of darkness appeared to Alenka's left and she knew that she had reached the pipe. She crept her way around the bend, all too aware that the worst part of the journey now lay ahead of her. At one point the tunnel was home to a number of light bulbs that helped make the journey more tolerable but now there was just the one - it was all too easy to knock against them and replacing the broken ones was a tedious business.

Although Alenka wasn't claustrophobic, she didn't consider herself to be a natural mole either. The tunnel was now pitch black and all she could hear was the scraping of her shoes against the ground. Even though there was only one way she could actually go, it was easy to feel as though she was lost in the abyss - whether her eyes were opened or closed there was nothing but complete and utter darkness in every direction.

There was an odd thing that she had noticed about the tunnel: everyone always talked about it in hallowed tones and anyone eavesdropping on the conversations would think that it was some glorious pathway to heaven... yet in reality no-one actually liked it. In fact, some of them actually despised it and it was easy to see why. Alenka often wondered if the horrendous journey through the darkness was responsible for the steady flow of desertions that occurred. Once you were out of the ghetto it took a certain amount of bravery to willingly come back into it, and it was for this reason that the existence of the tunnel was kept a closely guarded secret. Several idealists had argued that it could be used to sneak families out but the rest of them had quickly quashed that train of thought - as honourable as it was to do that sort of thing, it wouldn't be long before the Germans caught wind of it and blocked the tunnel up.

After what seemed like a thousand lifetimes Alenka spotted a tiny pinprick of light coming down from the ceiling. She groped around in front of her and swore as her finger banged against the rung of a ladder. Her voice sounded hoarse and strained, and she rapped her knuckles on the wooden hatch that hovered just above her head. During the brief silence that followed she began to wonder if the entire world above her had vanished. The muffled sound of footsteps was music to her ears and all of a sudden the hatch was pulled open.

"Welcome back," said a familiar voice.

Alenka croaked something and began clambering up the short ladder. After spending so long hunched down, her body was stiff and her legs had gone numb. Hands reached down to help her up, and she rolled over onto her side once she was over the top. The bright light hurt her eyes so she just lay there for a minute or so to recover.

She felt a gentle hand on her shoulder. "You alright?" the same voice asked her.

Alenka nodded weakly. She had done her fair share of guard duty for the tunnel, and was more than familiar with how people looked when they first emerged out of it. Their faces would be pale and panic-stricken, whilst the pupils of their eyes were stretched so wide that it made them look like demons. Some people came out shivering and shaking, but it was never from the cold. It wasn't even uncommon for some to shed a few tears.

Once she had sufficiently recovered Alenka slowly stood up. The cellar on this side was almost identical to the one she had come from, and for a moment she wondered if she had actually made it across.

"Ready to go up?" the man asked her.

Alenka nodded, followed him up the stairs and stepped into civilisation. The building this side of the tunnel was completely different to the one on the other side: the carpets were clean, the wallpaper was smooth and straight, and the smell of human excrement was non-existent. Although some had suggested that this was all an extravagant vanity that they couldn't afford, it was vital that appearances were maintained. At any time a postman, milkman, or a policeman might catch a glimpse of the inside of the house, resulting in awkward questions being asked if they spotted someone dressed in rags wandering around. Equally, the comings and goings of those inside the building had to be strictly controlled. Things had to look as normal as possible so letting everyone come and go as they pleased simply wasn't an option.

A woman came down the stairs and greeted Alenka. "Ah, you're just in time. The bedroom is all ready and there's clean clothes in the wardrobe. Go and have a bath if you like."

Alenka thanked her and went to the bathroom. She ran the bath so that the water was as close to scalding as she could stand; her teeth were tightly clenched as she gingerly lowered herself into it. At first she was happy to just lie there and let the water slowly work its way into her filthy, aching pores. She leisurely coated herself in soap and shampoo, massaged her feet, and lay back to enjoy the luxury of being clean while it lasted. Once the water began to cool down she stepped out and wrapped a towel around her waist. After scooping up her clothes she unlocked the door and tip-toed across the landing to the spare bedroom. She shut the door and sat down on the bed, relishing how soft and firm the mattress felt. The blankets and sheets were spotless, whilst the ceiling was free of cracks and cobwebs. After patting herself dry she lay down on the bed for a short nap. When she woke up, Alenka checked in the wardrobe and got herself dressed again. The clothes were simple and unremarkable but they were clean and pleasant to wear.

The room had a single window and she approached it with a degree of trepidation. The street below was devoid of the dead and the dying, and the gutter was free of blood and excrement. Although she couldn't see it from here, Alenka knew that the Ghetto Wall was lurking just around the corner and for reasons she couldn't quite explain, she hated looking at it from this side of the city - it seemed to stare at her like a gormless flat monster that was slowly inching its way across the world and eating everything in its path.

She went downstairs and asked if it was okay if she popped out for a while. Luckily things had been quiet all day, so she was free to go providing she stayed out for at least an hour. Alenka opened the front door and glanced up at the sky. Although she knew how ridiculous it sounded, even the weather seemed to be better on this side of the wall. She made her way along the streets, forcing herself to walk at a leisurely pace. It was nice being able to go about her business without having to worry about being bludgeoned to death. Along the way people nodded and smiled pleasantly at her, which was a comforting change from having people begging her for money and food.

She stopped outside a butcher shop and marvelled at all the different cuts of meat that were on display. The sausages looked a bit thinner and the steaks didn't look as lean as they had before the war started a few years ago, but it seemed that none of the people in the queue were any the wiser.

When she walked past a bakery the smell of warm sugar and birthdays wafted around her, and the iced ring doughnuts in the window looked like rows of heavily glossed lips. A serving girl leaned forward to pick up a chocolate eclair and a blob of cream fell off and plopped back down onto the counter. Alenka wondered how much of this food would be thrown away at the end of the day.

There was a cosy coffee shop just around the corner and Alenka couldn't resist popping in for a sit down. She ordered the cheapest coffee they sold and decided to treat herself to a small pastry as well. There was a free seat over by the window, one that she managed to claim just before someone else did. She slowly stirred her coffee and stared aimlessly out of the window watching people go by. Every passing face was pink and healthy, and every pair of hands were fleshy, full, and free of boils and sores.

Out the corner of her eye, Alenka could feel the admiring gaze of a German soldier who kept trying to catch her eye. He smiled pleasantly at her but she quickly looked away again - if they had been on the other side of the wall, he wouldn't have even given her a second glance.

On the way back to the house Alenka stopped outside a clothes shop. Six mannequins were impeccably dressed in luxurious outfits, all of them looking confident and assured in their expensive garments. She yearned to step inside the shop and feel the new fabrics rub against her skin, to have commission-hungry assistants make a fuss about her, and to look at herself in the mirror.

It was getting dark when Alenka finally arrived back at the house and she was welcomed by the aroma of a hot meal being prepared in the kitchen. The three of them ate together in the dining room and shared a bottle of wine, whilst a radio played pleasant music in the background. At first they talked about the war and the ghetto in general, but Alenka couldn't resist mentioning the clothes she had seen in the shop window. After five minutes of listening to them talk about fashion, the man rolled his eyes at the two women and went upstairs to read a book.

The wine and the food made Alenka feel drowsy and she gladly slipped in between the sheets once she was upstairs in her room. She buried her face in the pillows and laughed as her nose

112

was filled with the smell of fresh linen. It wasn't long before she was fast asleep.

The next morning she was awoken by the tantalising smell of eggs and toast, and after getting washed and dressed she went downstairs for breakfast. They were joined by a fourth person that Alenka recognised and she could tell from the strained look on his face that he had come through the tunnel.

"Haven't seen you for a while, Borys," she told him, trying to hide a smile. "Thought you were dead."

"Nah, you can't keep a good dog down. And I'm the best dog there is," he replied.

"Yeah, you smell like one as well."

Once breakfast was over the new visitor disappeared upstairs to the bathroom, and Alenka felt a pang of regret as she realised that the fun part of her stay on the Aryan side was over. Half an hour later Borys came back down looking clean shaven and wearing fresh clothes.

"Right, fancy a drive out into the country then?" he asked.

Alenka put her red cap on. "Ready when you are."

"You city girls look gorgeous when you dress up. Can we pretend we're married?"

"If you insist."

"Oh, I do. If anyone follows us we can pull over and get cosy just to throw them off."

"Silly boy," she replied. "If we're married, it means we hate each other."

Borys winked at her and opened the front door. Alenka followed him and they got into a black car that was parked over on the other side of the road, causing her to wonder if the vehicle had been there the day before when she went out for a walk. The start of their journey took them within sight of the Ghetto Wall and Alenka felt a knot of sickness in her stomach. She asked herself why they were bothering with all this cloak and dagger nonsense when they could just smash the wall down by driving into it.

"That thing gives me the creeps," Borys said, pointing at the wall. "It wouldn't surprise me if they started putting gargoyles along the top of it."

It took ten minutes for them to reach the edge of the city and every moment of it was a tense one. Alenka felt trapped and vulnerable inside the car, and every time they turned a corner she felt sure that a German soldier was going to yank open the door and drag her out into the street. When she had been walking around by herself it was easy to blend in with the crowd - there were all kinds of twisting alleys to hide down and she could even pretend to be a Dutch tourist if someone began asking too many questions.

Once they were beyond the city limits and the bricks began to make way for grass, Alenka started to relax. They drove through a small village and had to slow down for a chicken that was standing in the middle of the road. A woman sweeping leaves in her front garden looked up and eyed them suspiciously for a moment.

The journey continued for another twenty minutes, ending when Borys took a left turn up a well-worn dirt track. They came to a flat area that couldn't be seen from the main road.

"Okay, we're here," Borys said. He pulled a bit of paper out of his pocket and unfolded it. "This is a rough map of where the meeting place is."

Alenka looked at the piece of paper and saw that Borys wasn't exaggerating when he said it was rough.

"You go up this path here in front of us," he continued. Borys explained the route and asked Alenka if she had any questions. She shook her head and got out of the car.

"Goodbye, dearest husband," she quipped just as she closed the door.

Alenka turned and began walking towards the trees. The air felt colder under the shade and she shoved her hands into her jacket pockets. When the path split in two, she had to double check with the map to make sure that she was going in the right direction, whilst off in the distance the faint sound of a barking dog made her realise how alone she was. She stopped in the middle of the path and listened for any signs of life: there was nothing other than the sound of the wind blowing through the trees and the occasional songbird. When she closed her eyes and breathed in through her nose, she was reminded of how beautiful the world could be. Alenka let out a sigh and resumed walking at a slower pace. She plucked a leaf from a low hanging branch and wondered if there was a lake nearby. As a young girl she had always enjoyed

114

making little leaf boats and watching as they slowly floated away. Her brother would always try to sink them by throwing stones, no matter how many times she yelled at him.

Alenka grabbed at other leaves and branches, and soon her hands were covered in sticky sap. She clenched and unclenched her fists, smiling to herself as the residue bonded her fingers together. After walking for another twenty minutes she came to what looked to be the meeting place. To the left of the clearing was a rundown wooden cabin and a quick inspection revealed that there was only the one door secured shut by a twig. She decided against going inside as the lack of windows meant she wouldn't be able to see when someone approached it.

Over on the other side of the clearing was an old log that looked far more inviting so she slowly approached it and sat down. She glanced around, looking up at the tall trees and watched as a bird fluttered its way from one side of the clearing to the other. Alenka ran her hand over the log and bits of old bark flaked away from beneath her fingers. She carefully peeled off a larger piece of bark and watched as a family of woodlice scattered in all directions.

A sudden loud noise startled her and moments later a magnificent wild stag burst into view and stopped in the middle of the clearing. Alenka let out a small gasp and her eyes were wide with fear and wonder as the stag lowered its head to graze in the long grass. A few seconds later it seemed to catch her scent and it raised its head and looked directly at her. The stag's antlers were enormous and deadly, yet Alenka couldn't take her eyes off them. They were like two gigantic hands reaching up to the heavens and could probably kill her in an instant. Alenka wondered what she would do if it suddenly charged at her - would she hide behind a tree until it went away or would she just stand there and let herself be slain? Exactly what did she have to live for? Surely it was better to be gored by beauty than executed by a German bullet.

The stag darted off and crashed back through the undergrowth. Alenka watched it go and the world fell silent once again. She closed her eyes and wondered what it was that she was doing here - it would be so easy for her to just walk away and disappear forever. The thought of going back through the tunnel and returning to the ghetto filled her with dread.

After waiting patiently for another five minutes, she heard another noise over to her right. Two men appeared at the edge of the clearing and walked towards her. Alenka stood up as they approached, suddenly feeling alone and vulnerable. She glanced up at the sky and mumbled a quick prayer to herself.

"Hey," one of them gruffly greeted her. "You the one who wants some toys for her boyfriend?"

The man was overweight and ugly, and Alenka disliked him instantly. "Yes," she replied. "I told him that there's a wall of expectation that he needs to break down if he wants us to stay together."

Alenka hoped that they wouldn't have to continue speaking in code for much longer.

"Okay, Jew girl," the ugly one said, smirking at her. "Let's get down to business. I'm Achym and this is my friend Bach."

Alenka shook hands with the two men. She was sure she recognised Bach but couldn't say exactly where from. This wasn't the first time she had met up with smugglers and wannabe gangsters - no doubt they chopped and changed from one gang to the next depending on who was paying them the most money.

"What do you want from us?" Achym asked.

"What can you supply us with?"

He rolled his eyes in annoyance. "Whatever you want. Clothes, books, and beer if that's all you're after. Guns, bullets, and whores if that's more your style."

"Guns and bullets is a good start. Pistols are good but we've got some already. Rifles and machine guns would be better."

Achym threw his head back and laughed at her. "Ah, such a sweet girl," he mocked. "And where do you think I can get all these things? I can't just click my fingers and produce them from my backside."

A rush of annoyance ran through Alenka. "So what're you doing here, then? There's plenty of others I can go to."

Achym wagged a finger at her. "Sure, but they might not want to help you either. Tell me, why should we sell you anything?"

Alenka shrugged. "Because we need the weapons and we can pay you for them."

"Hmmm, it's not just the money that concerns us. What're you going to do with these toys if we give them to you?"

"The Germans are shipping us off to death camps," she said, trying to keep calm. "Innocent people are being killed and we need these guns to fight back."

Achym shrugged. "See, this is my problem: how do we know you will even fight? We know about these camps, and we watch you Jews going meekly and willingly to your deaths every week. No-one raised a finger when all those sweet little children were shipped off to the gas chambers."

Alenka didn't need to be reminded about what happened to the children from the orphanage. She walked past it nearly every day and it was nothing more than an empty shell now.

"There's plenty of us that want to fight. More and more of us every day but without weapons we're powerless."

"Okay, say this is true. What will you Jews do once you're free? Go home?"

Alenka pulled a face. "Why do you care?"

"I care because soon we'll have our own battles to fight. Poland is surrounded by invaders and we'll be fighting our own wars soon. It's not just the Germans who worry us, it's the Russians as well."

Alenka hadn't even considered this and she struggled to find a satisfactory answer. "Some of us have no homes to go to anymore," she replied. "There'll be plenty willing to join you afterwards."

Achym nodded slowly and considered her response for a few moments. "Let's hope so. What weapons do you need from us? We can get grenades, rifles, and machine guns quite easily. Landmines and explosives are trickier and more expensive. If it's tanks and planes you want, I suggest you send a nice letter to Winston Churchill in England."

The discussion continued for another twenty minutes. Alenka had no real idea what the weapons were actually worth - nor did she know what sort of funds were actually available to them inside the ghetto - but she was no stranger to bartering and striking deals.

At the very end of the meeting, Bach finally decided to say something and pointed down at Alenka's wrist. "You were wearing a watch last time I saw you."

Alenka frowned and glanced at her arm. "I was hungry so I had to sell it," she explained. "The man at the market took pity on me when I told him it was a family heirloom. He gave me two potatoes instead of one."

Bach narrowed his eyes at her, his expression a mixture of pity and amusement. Achym's face remained impassive. Before they departed the two men shook hands with Alenka and thanked her for her business. She had to suppress a smile when they realised that their hands were all sticky with tree sap.

Alenka watched Achym and Bach disappear into the woods and remained where she was for another ten minutes. Her freedom was quickly coming to an end and she saw no reason why she shouldn't savour it for a short while longer. A squirrel appeared and ran up the trunk of a tree, startling a bird into flight. Shortly afterwards she felt something on her fingers and looked down to see a woodlouse creep across her hand and slip under a piece of loose bark.

For her journey back to the car Alenka walked at a leisurely pace and she didn't bother to consult the map. Although she could remember the route well enough, there was a small voice in the back of her mind telling her that getting lost out in the woods was better than being in the ghetto. Eventually she found Borys sitting on an old wooden bench, his feet surrounded by discarded cigarette butts.

"You were gone a long time," he said.

"Yeah, those gangster types love the sound of their own voices."

"Did you find the place alright?"

Alenka nodded but didn't say anything.

"These woods are great, I used to come here a lot as a kid," Borys told her.

"It's beautiful here," she admitted. "Really, really beautiful."

She sat down next to him on the bench and waited for him to finish his cigarette.

"So we all sorted then?" Borys enquired. "You got good news for our friend Stefan?"

"Plenty of good news, yes. We've got pretty much everything a self-respecting resistance group could ever want coming our way."

Borys raised his eyebrows. "Everything?"

"Everything," she confirmed. "Well, apart from a postcard of the Taj Mahal."

A small frown appeared on Borys' face. He slipped his arm through Alenka's. "How about we celebrate like all the best married couples do? It'll be nice and warm in the car."

Alenka untangled her arm from his, readjusted her cap and stood back up.

"Boys," she muttered, rolling her eyes.

\*\*\*

## Chapter 9

The past four weeks were something of a blur for Abigail. Her memory of standing there in the street watching the children from the orphanage marching off to their deaths was clear enough, but everything afterwards was hazy and muddled. Although she didn't remember the journey back to the apartment, Leo had said that he picked her up and carried her back to her bed. She had spent the three days after that in an endless cycle of sleeping, waking up and crying, and back to sleeping again. Since then she had spent most nights sleeping in Leo's bed for warmth and comfort.

A week ago Abigail decided to start venturing out into the ghetto again. The silence inside the apartment when she was on her own was becoming unbearable and she needed something to take her mind off things. For some reason she found herself drawn towards the Ghetto Wall - there was something fascinating about the way its smooth pale face stretched for miles in either direction. In some places it even cut across tram tracks and roads, almost as if it had been lowered into place by a huge crane. It reminded her of when she would play in her back garden at home, placing her hand in the way of ants making their way across the patio. She would spend what seemed like hours trying to herd as many of the insects together as she could.

Looking up into the sky, Abigail searched for any signs of life but all she could see was an endless supply of white and grey clouds blocking out the sun. The longer she looked up at them, the more the clouds themselves began to look like an impenetrable wall that was built to stop anything escaping out to whatever lay beyond them.

Abigail reached out and touched the wall, only to find that it was as cold and unyielding as it had been the day before. She ran her fingers along it, feeling all the bumps and sharp edges of the bricks and cement. She came upon a set of tram tracks that disappeared under the wall and gently placed her hand on one of the rails. Although the dull steel was even colder than the wall, it felt as smooth and straight as a pane of glass. A strange sensation ran through her fingers and it took her a few moments to realise that the track was vibrating. There was a loud rumbling sound as a passing tram roared by on the other side of the wall and Abigail kept her hand where it was until the noise faded away. She wondered if there was anyone on the other side of the wall doing the same thing that she was: searching for signs of life.

Abigail stood back up and brushed the dirt off her fingers, flinching back as three German trucks roared around a corner and disappeared off into the distance. There seemed to be more trucks on the roads these days and she wondered what was going on. The soup kitchen was full of gossip these days but the more people talked, the more Abigail tried to shut it all out.

As she continued following the wall again, it wasn't long before she came to a section of the ghetto that she hadn't been down before. She stopped for a moment, teetering on a knife edge as she contemplated whether to go exploring or stick with what she knew.

Abigail decided to go exploring. As she made her way along the new street, Abigail saw that this part of the ghetto wasn't much different to the rest of it. The gutters were filled with the same filth that she saw elsewhere and some of the people she passed were little more than pathetic wretches. A large rat appeared from somewhere and darted across her path. Abigail watched it scurry off down an alley, briefly wondering whether she should follow it. She had never seen baby rats before so it would be interesting to find out if they looked like mice. There was a crossroads and she paused as the sound of another oncoming truck could be heard from around the corner. As she waited for the way to become clear, four people slipped out of a building over on the other side of the road. At first Abigail thought that they were also waiting for the road to clear, but the girl at the front crouched down and peered cautiously round the corner. As the roar of the truck became louder and louder, Abigail saw that one of the people over on the other side was waving frantically at her. A heartbeat later she realised that it was Leo and took a small step towards him. Leo's waving became more frantic than ever and Abigail realised that he was trying to wave her away. She shifted herself backwards and watched as the girl in front of him threw something small into the middle of the road. It was a round object that could have been a potato but it made a strange *clink! clink!* sound each time it bounced. The roar of the approaching truck was now so loud that it seemed to rattle Abigail's bones and a wave of fear rushed through her as she got the unmistakeable feeling that something bad was about to happen. After shuffling backwards a few feet she found herself huddling inside a doorway and she took a deep breath, wondering if it would be her last. The next few moments that followed were monstrous and confusing.

A German truck suddenly shot into view and hit an invisible barrier of some kind that had been placed in its way... or at least that is what *seemed* to happen.

There was a huge noise as the rear of the truck bounced into the air and came crashing back down again. A tyre flew off and disappeared down an alley somewhere, reminding Abigail of when she was at the circus watching a clown's car falling apart. The truck lurched drunkenly to the right and then back to the left, before toppling violently over onto its side. A number of soldiers tumbled out of the back, some of them shouting and screaming whilst others weren't moving at all.

When she heard the sound of joyous cheering, Abigail once again thought she was back at the circus. She glanced across the road and saw a small group of people jumping up and down with delight. One of them pointed a pistol in the direction of the truck and fired it twice.

Abigail looked back down the road and saw that two soldiers were trying to stand back up. A third was leaning against the underside of the truck, his left leg twisted and bent as if he had somehow grown an extra knee joint. His body suddenly jerked as if he had been hit with something heavy and he collapsed to the ground face first. A dark pool of liquid seeped out from underneath him, gliding quickly across the ground as if it were trying to escape.

Abigail was startled by the whine of a ricocheting bullet, and for some reason bits of masonry and brick were crumbling off the building behind her. She looked up and saw that a hole had somehow appeared in the wall. Two more holes suddenly appeared and Abigail shrank away from them. Several more holes appeared and she began to wonder if there was an invisible person smashing a hammer against the building to try and scare her away. As the holes crawled their way towards her, everything began to taste of dust and grit. Her ears were filled with the sounds of gunfire and screaming, and the invisible hammer began to bear down on her.

Someone from over the road lobbed another round potato towards the truck. It bounced twice, making a *clink! clink!* noise and the entire world fell silent. One of the soldiers lying on the ground grasped for it but his flailing hand couldn't quite reach it. He let out a low wailing that quickly built up into a scream as he realised that his life was rapidly coming to an end. There was a loud explosion and the soldier's body jerked like a twitching puppet. As the dust and haze settled, Abigail wondered why the soldier didn't seem to have a head any more.

The world turned silent again and Abigail hoped that the man with the hammer had been scared away. Someone began running across the road towards her and she let out a small whimper as a strong hand grabbed her by the arm.

"Abbie? What're you doing here?"

She looked up into the person's face and realised it was Leo. When she tried to speak all that came out of her mouth was dirt. A few minutes ago she had been doing nothing more than following the Ghetto Wall and doing some exploring - what on earth had *he* been doing?

"Come on, we've got to go," he said, helping her up. "More Germans are on the way."

Abigail followed him across the road and caught sight of someone lying on the floor. There was a dark red spot on one side of his head, and a pool of blood was drying underneath him. His eyes were open but utterly vacant.

"Is he...?" she asked.

The sound of German vehicles could be heard somewhere in the distance. Leo grabbed her by the arm and yanked her towards him.

"Come on!" he demanded.

Abigail glanced to her left and saw several soldiers lying on the ground next to the overturned truck. The only movement was from one of the rear wheels, spinning and turning as though the driver were still trying to accelerate away from all this madness.

As Leo dragged her into an alley, Abigail heard a gunshot somewhere behind her. She didn't dare turn to look but the crash of breaking glass sounded very close. Leo took a right turn and then a left turn. Abigail's arm was getting sore and she was glad when her brother stopped in front of a door and banged his fist on it. A moment later the door opened and Leo dragged her inside. When the door was closed shut again everything seemed dark and gloomy. Abigail's eyes were wide and full of fear, and her head spun as she tried to make sense of everything that had just happened. A pair of arms pulled her up against someone's chest and there was the sound of heavy breathing in her ear.

"That was close. We could've died out there," Leo told her. He leaned back and looked down at her. "What were you doing there anyway?"

"Nothing. I was just exploring," she replied in a small voice. "What were you doing?"

Leo opened his mouth and shut it again. He kissed her on the forehead and smiled. "Come on, I'll show you."

"Alenka's upstairs," said a voice behind Abigail.

Leo nodded and took his sister by the hand. As they went up the stairs, Abigail glanced behind her to see who it was that was following them. She got a glimpse of a broad-shouldered man who smiled at her.

"I'm in here!" announced a female voice.

Leo paused at the top of the stairs as he tried to figure out where the voice had come from. He went through the door to his left and into a room that overlooked the street below. A girl with blonde hair was peering out the window and in her hands was a rifle. She turned around as the three of them walked in.

"Where's Lem?" she asked. Her eyes flicked between Leo and the other man, before finally resting on Abigail. A frown appeared on her face.

"Lem didn't make it," Leo told her.

"Oh," replied Alenka. She pointed at Abigail. "Who's she?"

Leo bristled at the way the question had been asked. "This is Abigail, my sister," he replied, giving her hand a reassuring squeeze.

Although Alenka's expression softened she didn't say anything. Her head nodded slowly as if she was considering something, whilst the other man stepped out from behind Leo and held his hand out.

"Pleased to meet you, Abigail. I'm Borys. It's nice to have another girl with us, it evens the numbers up a bit."

Abigail glanced up at her brother questioningly, who gestured with a nod towards Borys.

"Nice to meet you, Borys" she replied shyly. His outstretched hand looked enormous and she was unsure about shaking it.

"Come on, Abigail," Borys said, smiling. "Don't be shy, I won't hurt you,"

Borys' friendly manner caused her to smile back at him and her cheeks turned a slight shade of red. She put her hand into his and was surprised at how gentle he was.

"There we are," he said, shooting her a quick wink. "You look so much prettier than your brother when you blush."

Abigail let out a surprised giggle and glanced back up at Leo, who grinned down at her.

"I'm Alenka," interrupted the blonde girl, who was now wearing a red cap. She offered nothing more than a weak smile.

"Hello," Abigail replied, sounding unsure of herself again. She thought she recognised Alenka but couldn't say where from.

The sound of two German trucks roaring past the building put an end to the introductions. The four of them all moved towards the window, though Abigail was stuck at the back and couldn't see anything. There were a few seconds of silence.

"What... what're they doing?" asked Borys.

"Looks like they're rounding people up," Alenka told him.

Leo glanced round and spotted his sister trying to find a gap to see through. He brought her round in front of him and rested his hands on her shoulders. Although Abigail could now see what they were all looking at, she still wasn't any the wiser about exactly what was going on. Further down the road a line of German soldiers had blocked off a section of the street. A few seconds later, two more soldiers led a group of people out of a building. A man stopped to readjust his shoe and received a heavy kick from behind. Some more soldiers appeared and used their batons to hurry the stragglers along.

A top-level window opened and someone poked their head out, almost as if they wanted to see what all the noise was about. The head jerked around a few times and a man suddenly tumbled out through the window, followed shortly afterwards by a set of crutches that clattered and snapped as they hit the ground. The man landed on his side and lay there on the pavement as he writhed around in agony, screaming when he caught sight of his twisted arm. A soldier walked up to him and gestured for the man to stand up. When the man didn't respond quickly enough, the soldier pulled out his pistol and shot him in the head.

Abigail let out a gasp and put a hand over her mouth. She felt her brother's grip tighten on her shoulders and someone else cursed loudly.

"Those gutless Nazi cowards!" fumed Alenka. "Let's see them try something like that on us!"

Everything was happening too far away for any of them to be able to do anything. As the buildings were emptied of people, the line of German troops moved further down the road and out of sight.

Alenka leaned back against a wall and slumped down to the floor. She put her head in her hands. "I can't believe this. We're right here and did nothing but watch it all happen."

"The Germans moved earlier than we expected them to," Borys reminded her. "Stefan warned us that this might happen. We've just got to be patient, they'll be using this road again soon."

Twenty minutes later, a German armoured vehicle roared down the street and stopped on the opposite side of the road. Abigail watched as a hand holding a bottle appeared from out of the open window across from them. The top of the bottle was on fire, reminding her of Christmas time at school - everyone in the class would bring in a bottle and paint it so it could be used as a candle holder.

The flaming bottle was thrown down onto the open-topped vehicle below. There was the unfamiliar sound of wet glass shattering, followed by a *wumph* and suddenly the entire vehicle was on fire. The loud, piercing screams of half a dozen soldiers sent a cold chill down Abigail's spine. Living columns of flame tumbled over the side of the vehicle and writhed around on the floor like upturned insects. Arms, legs, and heads seemed to vanish beneath boiling clouds of yellow and orange, only to reappear seconds later.

Alenka raised her rifle and pointed the barrel at the mass of soldiers. She aimed down the sight and found the head of a soldier who was sitting in the driver's seat. Her finger slid neatly and smoothly over the trigger... yet instead of firing the weapon Alenka suddenly found herself wondering how it had all come to this. As far as she was concerned, she was just another person trying to live her life so why was she aiming a gun at someone who didn't even know she was there? The soldier was just sitting there in the front cab of the vehicle, safe and sound from the inferno that was raging only a few feet behind him. He probably had a wife and a child, or maybe he was still a teenager living with his parents.

Alenka took a deep breath. Shooting painted targets in the woods was easy. Throwing a grenade into the path of an oncoming truck was easy. Talking about arming yourself and meeting up with gangsters was easy. Putting a bullet into an unsuspecting person's head was something she was completely unprepared for.

Alenka raised her head up from the rifle just as the armoured truck reversed its way back up the road. She pulled the trigger twice and felt the gun kick back against her shoulder. Two new holes appeared in the side of the building across from them, whilst other gunshots rang out and the screaming soldiers on the ground fell silent. She stepped back from the window, all too conscious of her sudden bout of cowardice, fully expecting Borys or Leo to snatch the rifle out of her hands so that it could be given to someone who was prepared to do what was necessary. Alenka was surprised - not to mention relieved - when she saw that everyone was too concerned with what was going on outside to be paying her any attention.

"That'll give them something to think about the next time they try anything like that again," announced Leo. "This is the turning point of the war."

Borys clapped him on the shoulder. "And we're right here at the root of it."

Alenka remained silent. The two bullet holes she had made seemed to be staring at her and mocking her. After all these months of being involved with the planning, the digging, and the scheming was her contribution to the uprising now at an end? She had been so sure of herself, so utterly convinced that when it came to doing what was required in the heat of battle she would be ready. How was everyone else able to stay so confident? Were the Germans always going to have the last laugh over her?

Abigail stared over at the building opposite them. Although she could see movement behind the window, the glare of the sun on the glass meant it wasn't possible to see any faces. She wondered just who it was over there and what they were doing. One of them had dropped a bottle of fire on the German soldiers, so she assumed that they were friendly. But were they soldiers themselves or just normal people with weapons?

Abigail's ears were still ringing from all the gunfire and the screaming, and her hands were shaking uncontrollably. There were dead bodies in the middle of the street below them, their faces and hands looking like freshly cooked slabs of meat. Although the flames had mostly died out there was still the occasional flicker of yellow as the uniforms burned away.

Abigail felt a dozen different emotions washing through her. The noises and smells of battle were alien and frightening, whilst the sight of people twisting and screaming as they fought to escape from the inferno raging around them filled her with dread - she had no idea it was possible for fire to stick to someone like that. And yet beneath all that, the only people who had been hurt were the Germans and it was the Germans who had brought them here. It was the Germans who were *keeping* them here. It was the Germans who were forcing her to live under a cloud of fear and terror, who made her shiver and suffer during the cold winter months, who made her feel hungry every single day - they were mean and nasty to her just like all those bullies at school were. In fact they were worse than the bullies because they had weapons, because they were strong, and because they were adults. The adults were supposed to protect her from the bullies and just as she had been glad when Leo had hurt the bullies, she found herself feeling glad that someone was hurting the Germans.

Everything about the past few minutes overwhelmed her and she turned away from the window. Leo was sitting down on the floor, talking with Borys who was sitting on the other side of the room.

Leo glanced at his sister and immediately saw that something was wrong. Her face was deathly pale and her eyes were darting nervously around the room.

"Abbie, come here," he said, reaching his hand out to her. She walked over to him as if she were in some kind of trance, and Leo pulled her down onto his lap. When he put his arms around her, he could feel her shaking.

"You alright?" he asked.

"I can still hear the screaming," she whispered. "Everything was so loud."

A tear fell down her cheek and Leo could see that her eyes were glistening wet. He stood up and led her out into another room and told her to sit down on the bed. She sat down and wiped her eyes dry.

"Who were those people in the other building?" she asked.

"They're friends of ours. They're on our side, fighting against the Germans."

Abigail's eyes widened. "Really? How many?"

Leo shrugged. "Hard to say. At least a hundred, probably lots more. There's other gangs fighting them as well."

"So are you all like soldiers in an army?"

Leo let out a small chuckle. "I guess you could say that, yes. We had to keep everything a secret so that the Germans wouldn't find out."

"Those people that were taken away," Abigail began. "Did they get sent to Treblinka?"

Leo nodded. He didn't like the direction that the conversation was taking but he was reluctant to hide the truth from her. "Yes. They're rounding other people up as well."

Abigail blinked. Her mind was beginning to follow some unpleasant threads of logic and a cold chill ran through her.

"What about Mum?" she asked. "Where is she?"

A hard lump appeared in Leo's throat. He didn't have a real answer to that question. "I don't know," he said, his voice cracking.

A look of horror appeared on Abigail's face. "We've got to do something!"

Leo took hold of her hand. "Remember what I said about keeping things a secret from the Germans? They don't know about that soup kitchen so she'll be safe down there. There's other underground bunkers with enough food stocked up to last a few weeks," he told her. "There's even an underground tunnel that goes under the wall and comes up outside the ghetto."

Abigail's eyes widened. "Really? An escape tunnel? You mean that?"

"Yes," he confirmed, feeling relieved that he had given her hope. "It's how we got all the weapons and food smuggled in."

Abigail gasped and wiped at her eyes again. Although her head was still spinning, the things that Leo had told her served to lift her spirits. For the first time it seemed that they might finally be able to go home again. She looked down at her hands.

"I'm glad," she said in a quiet a voice.

"For what?"

Abigail looked back up at him. "I'm glad that we hurt the Germans. They're mean and nasty, they deserve it."

Leo was filled with sadness. As much as he agreed with what she was saying, it pained him to hear her expressing such thoughts. Abigail was his little sister who wouldn't hurt a fly and he hated the fact that she was caught up in the middle of the fighting.

"Abbie," he said. "After this is over, no-one is going to hurt you ever again."

She smiled at him. "Okay."

Leo nodded. "If you're tired, you can go to sleep in here if you want."

Abigail's head was buzzing too much for her to try and sleep. "No, I'm not tired." She paused and a look of doubt appeared on her face. "When we go back in, are they going to laugh at me?"

"No, of course not. If anyone upsets you, come and tell your big brother," he smiled. "I haven't washed my feet for weeks, I'll throw my socks at them."

Abigail let out a small giggle. She leaned forward and kissed her brother on the cheek. "Thanks, Leo."

He took her by the hand and went back into the room they had come from. Alenka was leaning against the wall by the window, while Borys was sitting on the floor.

"Anything exciting happen while we were out?" Leo enquired.

"We spotted some trucks moving around and heard some gunfire in the distance, but that's it so far."

"You okay now, Abigail?" Borys asked. "Don't feel bad for getting frightened earlier, everyone is the same. I'm twenty five and I was scared when all those bullets were flying around. Same for those people in the building opposite us, your brother, and even Alenka here."

Abigail raised her eyebrows in surprise. "Really?"

"Sure, but they probably won't admit it," he smiled. "You saw what happened when we started shooting at those Germans. They drove off because they got scared. Stick a gun in someone's face and they'll soil their trousers, no matter who they are."

Abigail let out a nervous giggle, and Borys smiled at her again.

"Next time you get scared, just sit down here in the corner and put your hands over your eyes until it goes away. And if you get thirsty or hungry, there's probably a bit of food downstairs. There's a toilet in one of the other rooms and even a bed you can go to sleep on. Just make sure you don't fall asleep on the toilet like your brother does."

Abigail giggled again and glanced back at Leo, who was also laughing at the joke. There was even a ghost of a smile on Alenka's face as well.

"Actually, are you any good at first aid?" Borys asked.

"Um, my mum showed me how to tie a bandage," she replied. "And I know how to make a sling."

"Okay, that's good. If you see any of us bleeding anywhere, you can be our nurse if you want."

Abigail smiled and felt more assured about herself. She felt part of the team now, rather than being a scared bystander. "Sure, I'll do what I can."

"Good girl," Borys reassured her. "A soldier is nothing without a good nurse looking after him. You can even read me a bedtime story if you like."

Abigail giggled again, whilst Leo and Alenka let out small chuckles. The chat soon petered out after a while and the four of them sat there in silence. Aside from the occasional sound of gunfire or vehicles in the distance, the air was still. Abigail decided to take a look around the rest of the building while there was still enough sunlight and she was disappointed to discover that it was just a small residential place, with only a few rooms. Downstairs there was a kitchen and a small lounge, whilst upstairs consisted of the two bedrooms she had already been in and a cramped bathroom. There were a few tins of fruit that she brought up from the kitchen cupboards, along with a tin opener. She also found a pair of scissors and set about cutting up an old sheet into strips that could be used as bandages. There was nothing else for her to do, so she sat over in a corner of the room and let herself drift off into her own world as she worked. Abigail had no idea how long bandages were supposed to be, so she decided to make sets of them in two different lengths. After cutting a few strips out, she started rolling one up and realised that they needed something to stop them coming undone. Using the scissors again, she cut some short thin strips from the sheet that could be used to keep the bandages rolled up.

Alenka and Borys found it fascinating to watch her doing all this, with every bandage she created looking as immaculate and as straight as if it had been cut by a machine. Leo was more than aware of how skilled his sister was at this sort of thing but he still found himself impressed whenever she did something new. At one point Abigail disappeared from the room and returned with a chair so that she could practise tying the bandages around the legs.

As the day wore on, the four of them began to get hungry and they opened a couple of the tins that Abigail had brought up.

"Oh no, not peaches," groaned Borys. "I hate them, it's like eating slugs."

Leo exchanged an amused look with his sister. Abigail rinsed the tins out and brought them back full of water in case anyone was thirsty. As the evening wore on and the sky began to darken, the discussion turned to how they were going to organise the sleeping arrangements. In the end they decided it would be best if they all slept in the same room, so the mattress from the other bed was dragged in and placed onto the floor. Alenka volunteered to take the first shift on watch, whilst Borys agreed to take the second.

The end of a rope was thrown across to them from the window in the opposite building, and Abigail watched in amazement as a bag of supplies was sent over to them. Included in the bundle was a loaf of bread, a pistol, a candle and some matches. At Abigail's insistence three bandages were sent back.

When it came to finally settling down for the night, Borys volunteered to sleep on the mattress on the floor so that Leo and Abigail could share the bed in the corner. There was only one blanket and it was given to Borys. Within ten minutes the only sound in the room was the steady breathing of people sleeping, leaving Alenka all by herself.

The moon was high and full, and it seemed to be shining right through the window. Alenka looked up at its pitted surface, wondering if anyone had ever called it home. Perhaps there were people living there, looking down on planet Earth through giant telescopes. What would a civilisation like that think of their celestial neighbours? Would they be watching the events in the ghetto with horror, or would they be more interested in things like the Eiffel Tower and the Egyptian Pyramids? A cold chill ran through her and she turned her attention back to the people around her.

Although the room was dark, Alenka could just about make out some shapes around her. The door was nothing but an oblong of darkness and she couldn't quite tell if it was closed or not. It would be easy enough to take a few steps over to make sure, but a primal wariness of the dark kept her where she was. The candle that had been sent over lay somewhere nearby but she didn't want to risk attracting unnecessary attention from outside.

Next to the door was the mattress that Borys was lying on, a man whom Alenka considered to be a cheerful soul who often went out of his way to welcome newcomers to the resistance movement. He had a tendency to be a bit too persistent with the ladies - earning himself the unofficial nickname of 'sex pest' - but it was always nice to have him as part of the team.

Up on the bed lay Leo and his sister. The first time she bumped into Leo, he had been picking a fight with a small group of the so-called Jewish Police. The inhabitants of the ghetto who chose to join the Jewish Police found themselves in the unenviable position of being despised by both the Germans and everyone else around them. In exchange for this they got to wear a white band on their arm and were given a few extra rations each week. Although they were granted a small amount of power and authority, no-one actually took any notice of them unless they were backed up by German soldiers. Those that tried to abuse their position of power were prone to finding themselves dragged down an alley and beaten, whilst it wasn't uncommon for the worst offenders to have their throats slit open.

Once Alenka had begun talking to Leo, it didn't take her long to realise that recruiting him to the cause was going to be easy. Like many of their members, he was angry and thirsty for revenge but completely directionless; he acted as though he could fight the war all by himself. Although he had been reluctant to talk to her at first, softening him up had been simple enough - after listening to his story she began dropping hints about there being a resistance organisation, whilst lipstick and flirting did the rest.

Since then, Alenka had found him to be one of the more interesting people in the group. He was young and idealistic; he could be streetwise and hopelessly naive at the same time; he could be stubborn and argumentative, yet agreeable and easily swayed at other times; but most of all he was loyal and committed to the cause, which was the main thing.

He wasn't a bad looking boy either, although she wasn't sure if she could put up with him for very long if they got romantically involved. In some ways they were too alike and she was a good four years older than he was, not to mention that his personal hygiene left a lot to be desired. There was also the fact that she was actively avoiding getting too close to anyone since she lost her own family. The Germans had decided to do a series of random deportations, something that Alenka had avoided merely by chance - she had been over on the Aryan side of the wall when it had taken place.

And lying right beside Leo was his younger sister, an unexpected – not to mention unwanted – addition that had been thrust upon their little unit. Alenka had been dumbfounded when she first saw the small, frightened little girl wandering in behind Leo. For a fleeting moment Alenka had been tempted to shove her back out into the alley, but she knew that she would have had one hell of a fight on her hands if she tried anything like that - Leo often talked about his sister and would be the first to admit that he was very protective of her. He had once confessed that she was the only person in his family that he felt close to.

Borys had, of course, done his best to make their new member feel welcome, and Alenka knew that she wouldn't get any backup from him if she tried to palm Abigail off onto someone else.

Alenka felt a pang of thirst and searched around on the floor for the tin of water that was somewhere nearby. Her finger brushed against something metallic and she was careful not to knock the can over. After taking a few gulps, Alenka remembered that using them as cups like that had actually been Abigail's idea and she had done a good job of keeping them topped up too. Alenka thought back to how eagerly Abigail had busied herself with cutting all those bandages up - in the blink of an eye she had switched from huddling up against her brother for protection, to being confident and engaged with what she was doing. Anyone watching her at work would assume that she had done it dozens of times before - there was hardly any wastage and every strip was as straight as a train track. When Abigail had started practicing tying the bandages around the legs of the chair, Alenka allowed herself to believe that they had a fully-fledged medic with them. The thought of getting hit in the arm or a leg didn't seem quite as threatening as it might have done otherwise.

Sitting there alone in the dark, Alenka wondered what Abigail's life would have been like if the war hadn't broken out. She looked as if she would grow up to be one of those pretty petite girls that men are so fond of, destined to be snatched up by a wealthy young man who would treat her like a princess. They would live in a large house with an equally large number of servants to cater to their every whim, with Abigail treating every one of them as if they were close friends. Once married, the two of them would raise a large family of five or six children and Abigail would dote over every single one of them. She would teach them how to cook, how to make things, and how to love each other. She would wince at every scraped knee, share in the sadness and sorrow whenever a favourite pet died, and shed tears of pride and joy when they left for school each morning.

135

Alenka felt a hint of what might have been bitterness run through her. Was she jealous of this timid young girl? On the surface there didn't seem any reason for her to be, but seeing Abigail huddled up against her brother like that made her yearn for a time when someone was willing to take care of her for a change. With an older brother looking after her whilst she is young, and countless courtiers chasing after her when she was older, Abigail was destined for a pleasant and simple life.

Alenka looked back out the window and saw that everything was still and silent. After taking another gulp from the tin can she saw that it was nearly empty; if Borys got thirsty on his watch he was going to have to refill it himself.

*\*\**

## Chapter 10

Abigail was the first one to wake up the next morning and for a few moments her head was filled with confusion. She was used to waking up in a gloomy, cramped place yet for some reason the room was filled with cheery sunlight. A few blinks later and the memories of the previous day slowly worked their way back through her sleepy mind. She sat up slowly and carefully, not wanting to disturb the others. After taking stock of things, it seemed that nothing exciting happened last night - Borys was still and silent on the mattress, whilst Alenka was slumped down on the floor fast asleep.

Abigail looked back at her brother and a small smile appeared on her lips - for some reason he managed to look scruffy even when he was asleep. The closest she could describe him was like a homeless bear who has been dragged backwards through a hedge. As she stood up, it occurred to her that Alenka had fallen asleep at her post.

Abigail crept out of the room and into the bathroom. She was relieved to discover that there was enough water pressure for her to have a quick wash, and afterwards she went downstairs to refill the tin cans again. When it came to quenching her own thirst, she was glad that the taste of peaches just about masked the staleness of the metal.

Out of the corner of her eye, the back door that Leo had dragged her through loomed large. Small strips of light streamed in near the bottom where the wood was chipped and splintered, causing Abigail to wonder how secure it would be if a dozen or more soldiers were standing on the other side. She placed her ear up against the door to try and get a feel for what might be lurking out there, but couldn't hear anything. The silence was utterly devoid of life - she may as well have tried to listen out for death itself.

Abigail made her way back up the stairs, making sure not to spill any water. She placed the cans gently on the floor, away from any stray feet that might knock them over by accident. Over in the building opposite them, she thought she spotted some movement through the window. Abigail pressed her nose up against the glass and squinted to get a better look, but couldn't really see anything. She looked down at the road below them and saw that the bodies of the German soldiers had been moved. Their boots were missing, as were their weapons and most of their clothes. A strange tingling sensation ran through her when she realised that the corpses had been looted during the night - although it struck her as an unpleasant and grisly thing to do, Abigail couldn't quite bring herself to feel sorry for them. None of those soldiers had shown any compassion towards the living, so why should she feel anything towards them when they are dead?

Something in the sky suddenly caught her eye, causing her to stop and stare as if she were watching a magician pull a rabbit out of a hat for the first time again. Abigail threw the window open, leaning out and waving her arms wildly to get the attention of those on the other side.

"Look! Look!" she shouted across at them, pointing up at the sky.

Someone opened the window and craned their head round.

"Look, right up there!" Abigail yelled, barely able to contain her excitement.

The other person shrugged and said that they couldn't see anything. Someone else in the room came up behind them and ushered them away, so Abigail turned around and shouted everyone awake. Once she saw that they were suitably roused, she turned back to the window and stared up towards the sky in wonder.

Up on top of one of the highest buildings of the ghetto, the freshly-raised colours of white and red fluttered and flew majestically in the wind. Against a backdrop of suffering and oppression, the national flag of Poland was a much-needed beacon of hope, glory, and freedom. Right next to it, the colours of white and blue rippled and waved just as gloriously. After centuries of prejudice and banishment, the Jewish flag of Israel stood firm as a statement of defiance and resilience.

Gasps and exclamations of delight came from behind her, but Abigail barely heard them. As she stared up at the overnight appearance of these two newly erected flags, the primitive emotions of nationalism, patriotism, and tribalism stirred within her. All at once she began to realise what it meant it to be a Polish citizen; all at once she understood the importance of her Jewish heritage and culture. But most of all she realised what it meant to be part of something, to be part of a group of people rather than being a terrified outsider standing on the fringes.

Abigail span around, her face alive with happiness. Someone grabbed her and suddenly the four of them were holding hands and dancing around in a circle. Leo somehow managed to trip over the mattress on the floor and Abigail screamed with laughter at him. One of the tin cans was knocked over and Abigail kicked it as hard as she could, cackling with wild excitement and euphoria.

As the morning wore on, news of the flags spread all throughout the ghetto as people leaned out of their windows, cheering and waving at each other.

Abigail looked up at them again just to make sure that they were really there. As they rippled and flexed in the wind, she realised that weren't just sheets of pretty cloth - they were living, breathing entities just like she was. She suddenly thought of her mother and wondered where she was. Was she safe underground somewhere? Had she seen these flags? Were they ever going to see each other again?

Abigail turned around. "Does this mean that the war is over?" she asked.

"No," replied Leo. "But right now, the Germans are wondering what hit them. Two days ago they had this place under tight control. Now their soldiers are lying dead in the street and the tide is turning."

Once the initial excitement died down, their attention turned to more mundane things. They opened up a couple of cans and had something resembling a breakfast. Abigail went downstairs to fill the tins back up with water and began making some more bandages. Alenka watched Abigail for a few minutes, mulling something around in her head before finally making a decision.

"Abigail?" she asked. "Have you ever fired a gun before?"

Abigail looked up, wondering if she had heard the question properly. "No," she replied in a small, anxious voice.

Out the corner of her eye, Alenka could see that Leo was frowning at her and she did her best not to meet his gaze. She picked a pistol up from the floor and held it out towards Abigail.

"Come here, I'll show you."

Abigail blinked and looked at the gun as if it was a mysterious object that had fallen from the sky. As far as she was concerned, guns had only ever existed as a concept - they were something that only soldiers and policemen would ever use, and it never occurred to her that she would be able to hold one in her hand in the same way that she could pick up a pair of scissors. She stood up and walked towards Alenka, never taking her eyes off of the weapon. Now that she was up close to it, the pistol seemed smaller than it should be. How could so much fuss and importance be placed on something that fits into the palm of your hand? When Abigail reached out for it, Alenka pulled her hand back.

"Okay, let me tell you a few things first," she began. "Never, ever point a gun at someone unless you're going to fire it. So no holding it in your hand and waving it around, just in case it goes off by accident. When you're not using it, point it at the floor or the ceiling. It's why people put them in their belts or their pockets."

Abigail nodded. She had no idea that war could be so complicated.

"This pistol is a Luger," Alenka continued. A smile appeared on her face. "It's a German gun, just like my rifle is. That means you'll be shooting the Germans with their own weapons that were made in German factories."

Alenka ran her finger along the rifle she was holding. "See these tiny white marks? They're stress fractures from the cold, which means this particular gun came from the Russian front. The Germans are losing the war and the retreating soldiers are throwing their weapons away."

Abigail's eyes were wide as she took this all in. Alenka stepped behind her and gently slid the gun into her hands. It felt cold, heavy, and bulky; it felt like death.

"Okay, this is how you hold it," Alenka told her, moving her fingers around. "Right, see that dark section on the wall down there? Aim for it and see how you do."

Abigail took a deep breath and did her best to point the gun in the right direction, but it was harder than it looked. When she focused on the wall, the gun seemed to move and wobble like a plate of jelly; when she tried to concentrate on the gun, the wall seemed to ripple and move like the wings of a butterfly. She clenched her teeth and tried to pull the trigger but found it too stiff. After realising that she had been trying to squeeze the entire thing like a sodden sponge, she readjusted her grip and tried again. There was a loud noise and the gun suddenly jerked and bucked around as if it were alive, and it was all she could do just to keep hold of it.

"Hmmm, not bad for a first go," Alenka told her. "I think you had your eyes closed though. Try it again."

Abigail's heart was thumping hard and her hands were shaking uncontrollably. A cold sweat had broken out on her face, causing her to wonder if she was going to faint. She looked at the wall and saw that a new hole had appeared, though it was nowhere near where she had been trying to aim for. She closed her eyes and took a deep breath. When she opened them again, she found herself looking up at the two flags and a feeling of pride settled over her. She took aim for a second try, this time making sure she kept her eyes open. The gun seemed to jerk the moment she touched the trigger and this time the hole that appeared in the wall was closer to where she had been aiming for.

"That's better," Alenka told her. "Have another go, you're getting used to it."

Abigail held up the gun for a third time and noticed that it didn't feel quite as awkward as it had done before, almost as if it had shrunk to fit her hands. The gun jerked again but this time she was ready for it, and the noise didn't seem as deafening either. Another hole had appeared on the wall, this one just outside of the area she was trying to hit. She was already setting herself up for another go when Alenka prompted her to try again.

By the time Abigail fired it a seventh time, the gun felt as if it was part of her hand. It no longer jerked around like a wild, untamed horse and the gunfire had simply become background noise.

"I'm impressed," Alenka told her, putting a hand on her shoulder. "You're quite the natural marksman."

Abigail looked over at the wall and saw that the man with the invisible hammer had been busy again. Fresh holes peppered the side of the building opposite them - there were two near the outside of the area she had been aiming for, along with a final one almost right in the middle. When she realised that those holes had been made by her own hand, Abigail was filled with a sense of pride and accomplishment. She raised the gun for another go and was surprised when she got nothing but an empty click.

"That's the Dead Man's Click," Alenka told her. "The magazine only holds seven bullets, so make sure you don't get caught out."

When Alenka took the gun away from her, Abigail wanted to snatch it back; she liked the feeling it gave her to hold it in her own hands. Alenka began explaining how to eject the magazine and what the safety catch was for. Abigail listened intently and was glad when the pistol was handed back to her.

"Keep it," Alenka told her. "No point leaving it lying on the floor if you can use it."

As Abigail nodded solemnly in agreement, Alenka tilted her head to one side as she considered something.

"Hold on," she said, fumbling around in her pocket. She brought out a black cylinder and twisted the bottom of it. "This one's practically new. No point letting it go to waste."

Abigail had never owned her own lipstick, but she had once crept into her mother's room to try some on. It turned out to be far trickier to apply than she had imagined it to be, and her mother had laughed when she saw the awkward red lines smeared all over her daughter's face.

Alenka expertly applied some to Abigail's lips, before tucking the cylinder back into her pocket. "There," she said. "You look like a proper Jewish girl now. A proper Jewish warrior princess!"

No-one had ever said anything like that to her before and Abigail beamed with pride. She turned around and saw that Leo was still sitting on the bed, his face full of anger. When his eyes flicked down to meet her gaze, his expression softened and Abigail stepped towards him, doing her best to hide a grin. She leaned forwards and kissed his cheek, giggling at the bright red imprint her lips left behind. Leo laughed and playfully pinched her nose.

"Hey, don't I get a kiss as well?" asked Borys.

Abigail turned around and beckoned for him to crouch down to her level. She planted a kiss on his cheek and giggled loudly.

"I've just been kissed by the prettiest girl in Poland," he announced. "Look, I'm blushing more than she is."

Abigail flushed a deep shade of red and giggled again.

"You're a top nurse, a natural marksman, and a beauty queen all rolled into one!" grinned Borys.

Once the laughter and jovialities had died down, Abigail retreated back to her corner and took the pistol out of her pocket. She ran her fingers all over the weapon, touching and sensing every screw and every bump so she could get a feel for it. Her hands stroked and caressed the metal, turning it over and over until it felt natural against her skin. She flicked the safety catch on and off several times, and practised releasing and reloading the magazine. The Luger belonged to her now and she wanted to master it like she had mastered scissors and paper at school. When she brought her hand up to her nose, her nostrils were filled with the smell of gun grease. The longer she looked at the pistol, the more assured she began to feel with it and a strange feeling ran through her, one that she didn't recognise - a feeling of safety, a feeling of security - for the first time in her life she had *power*.

Abigail thought back to all the times that Leo had had to rescue her from the boys at school. She thought back to when the Germans evicted them from their home, and she thought back to when the soldier had chased her as she carried Ham back to the orphanage. Most of all, she thought about how different things would have been if she had owned a gun - no-one would have dared to bully her as she played with the bees and the butterflies, and no-one would have dared to push her family around.

As Leo watched his sister fiddle with the gun, he felt a strange sickness wash over him. A pistol was a deadly weapon, a tool for warriors during times of war. His sister was his sister, a sweet little girl who was made for caring and creating rather than killing. It wasn't all that long ago that he had been dancing around the room with her on her birthday - was that innocent young girl gone forever?

Leo glanced over at Alenka. When she met his gaze, Leo suddenly felt angry with her. He glared at her for a moment before standing up and storming out of the room without saying anything. As soon as he stepped out into the hallway, he realised there was nowhere for him to go. He banged the underside of his fist against the wall and stomped his way into the bathroom. After making sure that the taps were still working, Leo splashed cold water over his face and sat down on the toilet seat. As his anger died down, he realised that what Alenka had done made sense - the more guns that they had firing at the Germans, the more likely they were to win. He splashed his face with water again and made his way back into the room where everyone else was. Borys greeted him with an amiable nod, whilst Abigail smiled sweetly up at him when he sat back down on the bed. It seemed that she had become bored of the pistol and was back to fiddling around with the bandages.

Leo purposefully avoided looking at Alenka: although he agreed with the logic of what she had done, it didn't mean he had to actually like it.

Twenty minutes later, Abigail was refilling the empty cans with water. As she set them down on the floor, the sound of gunfire drifted in through the window. Everyone quickly rushed over to see what was happening, with Abigail doing her best to squeeze her way to the front. An armoured vehicle was parked over on the side of the road, whilst a handful of soldiers peered out from behind doorways and corners. Abigail spotted one of them raise his rifle before firing it at a target that she couldn't see. Another soldier seemed to be looking right at her and for an absurd, fleeting moment she wanted to wave at him. There was a muzzle flash and something hard and heavy hit the window frame just below her, sending bits of wood and brick flying up into her face. She flinched back, wanting to run away from these awful soldiers with their evil guns. Her hand brushed against something hard and heavy in her pocket, and Abigail suddenly remembered that she had a gun of her own. She took it out and released the safety catch without even thinking about it, and as she raised the pistol to take aim another muzzle flash appeared from below. Something zipped through the air and passed over her head but Abigail wasn't scared this time, she was angry and thirsty for revenge. From behind her was the sound of someone crying out in pain, but she barely even noticed it. Abigail paused for a moment as she realised that she was about kill someone - was this really what she wanted to do? She thought of her father. She thought of Ham, Antoni, Janusz, and everyone at the orphanage. She thought of her mother. She thought of the boys who pushed her over at school and her finger slipped over the trigger and squeezed it twice in quick succession. Although the gun was still trying to jump out of her hand, she knew how to brace herself for it.

Abigail was vaguely aware of someone to the left of her firing a rifle but it was mere background noise. Down below on the street a soldier lay unmoving on the ground. A strange dark shadow began scurrying away from underneath him before Abigail realised it was his blood. Two new bullet holes had appeared in the wall that the soldier had been sheltering behind. So who had shot him? She, or the person beside her?

Another muzzle flash attracted her attention and Abigail took aim again. The gun jerked in her hand but the soldier stubbornly decided to remain where he was. When she pulled the trigger a second time, the soldier twitched violently and collapsed to the floor. More flashes appeared from various nooks and crannies, and Abigail shot at each of them in turn without even thinking about it. A soldier dashed across the road and she pointed the pistol at him.

*Click.*

*Click.*

*Click.*

Abigail's eyes widened as she realised that the gun magazine was empty. She suddenly felt powerless and afraid again, all too aware of why it was called Dead Man's Click.

"There's more ammo in the bag," Alenka yelled. She used her foot to shove a tattered cloth bag in Abigail's direction.

Abigail crouched down to fish out a new clip and the moment it clicked into place, she felt safe and powerful again. When she stood back up, a hunter's instinct rushed through her as she caught sight of a soldier scampering down the road. She fired at him twice, barely even noticing the recoil - instead of jerking and jumping, the gun seemed to merely vibrate in her hand; whereas once it had felt like trying to control a defiant bulldog, it now felt as meek as a rabbit.

A small smile appeared on Abigail's face as the retreating soldier collapsed to the floor and tried to crawl away. She fired at him again and he stopped moving completely.

There was the sound of a bottle breaking and the *wumph* of freshly ignited flames, followed by the kind of wild screaming that only someone whose face is on fire was capable of. A potato bounced down the road, making a strange *clink! clink! clink!* sound as it came to rest next to two soldiers. A loud explosion caused Abigail to blink and when she looked again, there were two dead soldiers where living ones had been standing only moments before.

The battle seemed to end as quickly as it started and Abigail's eyes darted from corner to corner looking for any remaining targets. As the silence stretched out, she became aware of how heavily she was breathing. The endorphins and adrenaline drained from her body, sending pulses of dizziness rushing through her. The street below seemed to be littered with dead bodies, smears of clotting blood, and discarded weapons. She looked down at her hands, not quite able to believe the part she had played in all this. Something moved at the edge of her vision and she looked up just in time to see a body being dragged round a corner. When she relaxed again, she saw that she had raised the pistol without even realising it.

"We scared them off again," said Alenka. "I bet they're cowering down in their holes wondering what hit them."

Abigail suddenly felt very self-conscious, wondering if they all thought she was an insane killer. She turned around and was relieved to see that no-one was paying her any attention at all. Leo was tucking his own pistol back into his belt, whilst Alenka rested her rifle against the wall. Borys was sitting on the bed, wincing in pain whenever he tried to move his arm. The top half of his shirt sleeve was wet with blood.

"What happened?" Abigail asked.

"I got shot," he told her.

Abigail blinked at him. "I can fix it," she blurted out. "At least, I think so."

Borys smiled at her, and she grabbed hold of some of the bandages she had made.

"Sit down there on the floor, it'll be easier," she told him.

Borys did as she asked and began unbuttoning his shirt. He shook his arm free of the sleeve, grunting with each movement.

Abigail looked at the wound and grimaced. It was smeared with blood and dirt, whilst the gash itself seemed to glisten with anger.

"Don't move, I'll need to clean it first," she told him.

Abigail grabbed hold of a can of water and used a bandage to wash Borys' arm. She dabbed lightly and expertly with the cloth, mindful of how painful it must be for him. From what she could see, the bullet had passed right through the fleshy part of his bicep.

"You were lucky," she told him.

"Sure, all the lucky people get shot."

Abigail giggled and began wrapping his arm up. She used two of the homemade bandages, just to make sure it was kept tight and protected. Now that she was up close to Borys, she could see that there was a red tinge to his hair. It reminded her of Antoni, sending a mixture of happiness and sadness through her. She leaned forward and planted a light kiss on Borys' cheek, leaving a faint red mark to match the one on the other side of his face.

"That's for being such a brave boy," she said.

Borys laughed loudly, but his mirth was quickly quenched when the movement hurt his arm. He placed a kiss on her forehead.

"That's for being such a wonderful nurse," he told her.

Abigail blushed and giggled. She thought of Antoni again, remembering that day when he had held her hand. Would things have been different if she had been wearing lipstick? Would a red imprint on his face have protected him from extermination? What would it have cost to buy a tube of lipstick? The orphanage always had plenty of food - she could have kept back a sausage or an apple, or maybe even stolen a bar of soap to trade with.

"Abigail? Are you okay?" Borys asked.

Abigail looked at him. "Call me Abbie," she said in a quiet voice.

An idea popped into her head and she picked up the scissors. Before Borys could say anything, she reached out and snipped off a small portion of his red hair.

"I want some of your good luck," she told him. It was only half a lie.

Borys laughed again. "Abbie, I think everyone could do with a bit of luck. Maybe you should cut some more off and share it around."

Abigail smiled and stood up. She opened her hand and looked at the small lock of hair she had taken. Although it hadn't actually come from Antoni's head, the faint redness meant it was the closest thing she had to remember him by. It also meant she would have something to remember Borys by, a man who had been kind and welcoming to her from the moment they first met. She put it into an inside coat pocket so that it wouldn't get lost. When she turned around, she saw that both Leo and Alenka were looking at her. There was a small but pleasant smile on Alenka's face, and a familiar brotherly look on Leo's.

"Good job, Abbie," he told her.

"Thanks," she said, feeling proud of herself.

"We should've brought you into our resistance group earlier," remarked Alenka.

Leo snapped his head round. "No, we shouldn't," he disagreed, suddenly annoyed with her all over again. "She's just a girl and shouldn't be involved in any of this."

Alenka rolled her eyes. "You know how desperate we were for good people. Your sister can wield a gun as easily as she dresses a wound, and picks things up quickly. She could even go through that tunnel faster than any of us would be able to. God gave her a gift, why should -"

"God had nothing to do with it," Leo snapped. "Everything she knows, she learnt it all by herself. What gifts was God blessing her with when she was being bullied and beaten at school?"

"It doesn't work like -"

"Yeah, he moves in mysterious ways," Leo interrupted. "So mysterious in fact, that he's about as much use to us as the tooth fairy. Look at us. Look at where we are, living in squalor and surviving on stale bread every day. How can you worship someone who treats us like this?"

"It's called faith," she hissed. "We trust in his judgement and do everything we can with what he gives us. Isn't there anything you believe in?"

"I believe in myself. I believe in humanity."

"Humanity?" scoffed Alenka. "It was the evil of humanity that dragged us from our homes in the first place. It's God that gives us the strength to fight back against the humanity that put us here."

"And it'll be humanity that gets us back out again," Leo retorted. "This war is raging across half the world now. People have seen the danger with their own eyes and are fighting back out of their own free will. Soldiers train and arm themselves whilst the priests and rabbis pat their books and mumble meaningless prayers."

"Don't be so stupid!" she shot back. "Those rabbis give faith and comfort to everyone who goes to them. People depend on them for hope and strength."

"Sure," leered Leo. "It's funny how none of those rabbis are ever starving and dying on the street like the rest of us. I've seen them with their gold chains and sparkling rings. Think how many people could be fed with such riches."

"You know nothing!" spat Alenka. "The value of those holy items goes way beyond their material worth. After you sell them and the money runs out, what then?"

"Then we go onto the next little stash they have hidden away. After that we move onto the parasites who makes themselves rich at our expense. You've seen the workshops, right? The owners get fat while the children work themselves to exhaustion just to buy a scrap of meat."

"That's just the way it is!" declared Alenka. "Where do you think the money for these weapons comes from? It comes from those rich people you despise so much. Without them, we would be throwing rocks and potatoes instead of bullets and grenades."

"None of them gave us anything until we started begging them. It wasn't until we threatened them that they actually began to take us seriously. They were all happy to keep things as they were."

"That's just the way of the world," she replied. "You take whatever you're blessed with and do the best you can."

Leo laughed at her. "And now you're back to justifying everything with God. Think for yourself instead of looking to some higher power all the time. You worship your god in the same way that they," he gestured with his hand. "worship their Fuehrer."

Alenka's face twisted in fury and for a fleeting moment she wanted to smash him over the head with the butt of the rifle. "How dare you compare me to those monsters," she snarled.

Leo didn't flinch but remained silent. A feeling of smug self-satisfaction settled over him as he saw how angry he had made her. The entire room remained still as they stared each other down.

"If it makes you feel any better," Borys interjected. "I'm not even Jewish."

Three sets of eyes swung round and stared at him in disbelief. "What?" Leo finally asked.

Borys let out a short embarrassed laugh. "I'm not Jewish," he repeated.

"So what're you doing here?" Alenka asked.

Borys sighed and took a moment to consider what he was going to say. "I'm homosexual."

Alenka shut her eyes as a thousand questions filled her mind. The stunned silence seemed to stretch on forever. "So... why tell us now?" she enquired. "Why the secrecy?"

Borys shrugged. "Life is hard enough in here as it is. Why would I want to make myself an even bigger target?"

"Right. But all the things you... how you act..."

He let out a small laugh. "Yeah, the flirting and bold propositioning. I know people call me Sex Pest in secret. Way I see it, it meant people wouldn't ask any awkward questions."

"So how did you end up here?" Leo asked.

Borys' face turned sad. "Same way you lot did - with a gun pointed in my back. On the day the evictions started in my town, I was just standing there on the side of the road like everyone else. Just... standing and staring. That's the worst part about all this, everyone just stood there watching it happen. No-one raised a finger, including me. I just stood there thinking 'poor bastards, glad it's not me' as they went past.

"Anyway, some woman walked up to me. There were two policemen following behind her, real ugly brutes who looked like they could eat their way through a brick wall if they had to. The woman, she pointed at me. 'This is the one I told you about' she told them. 'He's the queer who goes around doing disgusting things to animals and boys each night."

Borys' gaze was fixed on the middle of the floor. His expression was serious, almost as if he was going to cry.

"Who was she?" asked Alenka. She shifted her feet, feeling uncomfortable for asking the question.

Borys looked up at her. "I've got no idea; I'd never seen her before in my life. The look in her eyes though, it was just pure hatred and venom. I actually thought it was a joke until they dragged me up in the back of a lorry with everyone else. I looked to my neighbours for help but they just turned the other way. No-one wanted to help me, they were all too scared."

"Did you have a partner? Any idea what happened to him?"

Borys swallowed. "No idea. He's probably dead. I did try to find out, but..." he let the sentence trail off and rubbed his eyes. "Well, the support networks here only really deal with Jews. No-one knows who he is and I didn't want to risk making life harder for him."

Abigail had listened to Borys' story without saying anything. She didn't have much more than a vague notion of what sex was, with most of her knowledge coming from overhearing the whispers of the older girls at school. There were diagrams and pictures in the rear sections of the science textbooks, but for the most part it was all a bit of a mystery. Although she knew that boys and girls fell in love with each other, the details were hazy and confusing, whilst the notion of boys being in love with other boys was almost beyond her comprehension. She wondered what it meant in light of all the nice things that Borys had been saying to her. Abigail liked it when he joked with her and said that she was pretty. Did any of that change now that she knew he liked boys rather than girls?

She squeezed the pocket that held his lock of hair and a pleasant warmth ran up her arm. As far as she was concerned, it didn't matter who Borys fell in love with - he was still the friendly and funny person who said nice things to her. He had made her feel welcome when others wanted to ignore her. She bent down and kissed him on the forehead, leaving another red mark on his face.

"You're still my brave boy," she told him.

When Borys looked up at her, his eyes were glistening with happiness and sorrow. He reached out and took her hand.

"Abbie, you're the sweetest little thing I've ever met. If anyone deserves to survive this war, it's you," he gestured towards the others. "You're better than those two stubborn dogs any day of the week."

Leo and Alenka shifted uncomfortably and avoided looking at each other, whilst Abigail sat down next to Borys and patted his arm. He smiled at her and leaned his head back against the wall. A quietness seemed to descend on the world as Leo and Alenka did their best to pretend that the other didn't exist. Abigail and Borys talked in quiet whispers, with only the occasional small giggle breaking the silence.

A while later, a strange clanking, squealing noise began to filter in through the window. Leo and Alenka were the first ones to notice it and they looked at each other uneasily. Borys turned his head slowly towards the window, a look of despair settling on his face. The sound was completely alien to Abigail and in her mind all she could picture was a gigantic shadow slowly descending from the sky, ready to destroy everything in its path.

"What's that noise?" she asked. Her face was deathly pale.

"It's a tank," Leo announced.

This revelation actually made Abigail feel more at ease, and she stood up to take a look out the window. She had never actually seen a tank before, so all she could see was a large metal box without any wheels floating towards them. Bobbing up and down behind the tank were the heads of soldiers using it for cover. It was hard to see exactly why it was making such a loud clanking sound and she wondered if there was something bouncing around inside it. Abigail stepped back from the window and put her hands over her ears. The noise seemed to be rolling towards her and it was the most unnatural thing she had ever heard - it was as if the death camps had somehow come alive and were coming to take her away.

Leo's face took on a grimace, whilst Borys closed his eyes. Alenka looked out the window again, her eyes narrowing as if she were checking over a shopping list for something that she had missed. A strange smile appeared on her face, the sort of smile that someone pulls when they know something that no-one else around them does and her lips began to move as if she murmuring a quiet prayer. Just as the tank approached a loose section in the road, she screamed something.

All of a sudden, three enormous explosions went off one after the other. The noise was horrific and seemed to roll on and on like a relentless earthquake, and Abigail likened it to hearing the sound of three gigantic boulders plunging into the sea. It was as if the entire world were ripping itself apart, and the sound was bouncing off of everything that she looked at - it bellowed at her from the walls, from the floor, from her feet, and from the air itself. Her senses became overwhelmed and she struggled to see or breathe. Her vision returned in hazy fits and starts, and for some reason she found herself lying down on the floor. Although the noise seemed to have stopped the world was still filled with an endless sense of chaos. Leo had a dazed look on his face, whilst Alenka seemed to be out of breath and deliriously happy about something that only she could see. She was yelling something but Abigail couldn't quite make out what it was. Reality began falling back into place and Abigail could hear a familiar snapping, crackling noise. Alenka's mouth was still moving.

"...landmine... saw them put it there last night... invincible..."

Abigail stood up and tried walking to the window. Her legs felt heavy and she had to use the wall to stop herself from falling over. When she finally managed to peer outside vertigo washed over her, causing the ground to bounce up and down before her eyes. A twisted black shape was parked in the middle of the road, orange flames belching out of its sides. Thick black smoke rippled and boiled its way up into the sky, whilst the stench of burning diesel filled the air.

Abigail found herself mesmerised by the roaring crackle of the flames. She followed the path of the smoke up into the sky, catching sight of the Polish and Israeli flags fluttering away in the background. A smile appeared on her face as it dawned on her what had happened. She took a step backwards to tell everyone else the good news, only to tread on someone's foot. The four of them stood there in stunned silence and for the first time they allowed themselves to believe that they could do what everyone

153

else had failed to do: take on the might of the German army... and win.

***

Once the novelty of the burning tank wore off, the four of them turned their attention to other matters. Abigail was the first one to notice that the flags had sprouted a few holes.

"Bullet holes," Leo told her. "The Nazis always go for the easy targets, it's what their ideology is based on. If they want to trade their soldiers for bits of cloth, that's fine by me."

The smell of burning diesel began to make them feel sick so they decided to close the window, and Abigail gulped down several mouthfuls of peach-scented water to get rid of the acrid taste. As the sky began to darken, the rope was once again strung across from the building opposite them. Some food was sent over, along with a note saying that they might get the order to move locations during the night. They decided to keep the same shifts as before for keeping watch, though none of them mentioned that Alenka had fallen asleep last time.

Abigail and Leo shared the bed again, with Leo draping a protective arm over his sister. He lay awake for longer than he normally did, listening to the faint sound of her breathing and wondered how much of his little sister he was going to lose by the time the war ended. The past two days had already chipped away at her innocence - how much of a hammering could it withstand?

Leo couldn't actually decide if he was glad that she was with him or not. Although he wished she was safe in one of the underground bunkers, at least this way he could do his best to look after her. Despite what he had told her about their mother being safe in the soup kitchen, he knew that no-one was *truly* safe. It was possible for the shelters to be found using special equipment, or simply from other ghetto inhabitants telling the Germans in exchange for food. Leo let out a sigh and allowed himself to fall asleep.

At some point in the middle of the night, he was shaken awake again. Leo could have sworn that he had only just dropped off, but it was Borys' voice he heard.

"Come on, we need to move," he said in a whisper. "The Germans are trying to surround us."

Leo grunted and sat up, whilst Abigail whimpered somewhere below him and got up off the bed. She let out a small, child-like yawn that caused Leo's stomach to do a funny turn - it was pitch black outside and he was concerned about how vulnerable she would be once they stepped out of the building.

The four of them gathered up their things as quickly as they could. Someone knocked over a tin of water and Abigail wondered if she was ever going to taste peaches again. They crept down the stairs as quietly as they could, using their hands to guide them through the darkness and when they reached the back door, Alenka placed her ear against it.

"It seems clear," she whispered.

As she pulled the door open, there was a squeal of hinges that set their hearts racing. Alenka went out first as she was more familiar with where they had to go. Leo went second, with Abigail and Borys coming behind them.

The moon was high and bright in the sky and Abigail felt as if it was beaming directly down on them. Was the moon just another tool of the Nazi state, a puppet entity coerced into pointing out anyone who dared to defy them?

When Borys pulled the door shut behind him, the faint click of the lock made Abigail realise that there was no going back now, only forwards. Just as she turned around to follow her brother, she thought she spotted movement behind Borys. There was a strange hiss, followed by a bright flash and suddenly the entire alley was filled with light. And screaming. A horrific wild screaming that sent a chill through Abigail's heart.

Borys thrashed around wildly, bouncing from one wall to the other as the flames raced over his entire body. Somewhere behind him, a figure dressed in a shiny black material took a step backwards and pointed a long nozzle at the rest of them. The figure didn't seem to have a face, just an anonymous mask with round windows for eyes.

Abigail felt something zip over her head and the figure in black fell backwards. A thin stream of fire spurted out from the nozzle, smearing the side of the building with flames.

The world was now alive with the kind of light and heat associated with an Indian summer. Borys writhed around on the ground, his face all black and twisted whilst his screaming had turned hoarse and dry.

Abigail felt a strong hand grab her, one that nearly yanked her arm off. Leo pulled her along as they sprinted down the alley, taking her through what seemed to be an endless series of twists and turns. When they shot across a road without stopping to see if the way was clear, Abigail realised that the notion of sneaking out quietly had been abandoned entirely. They stopped suddenly and Alenka shoved open a door with her shoulder. The three of them tumbled inside, panting and sweating profusely.

A single candle stood in the corner of what seemed to be a kitchen. Abigail went to Leo, who put his arm around her. Alenka slid to the floor and leaned back against the wall. She put her head in her hands and let out a small wail.

"I can't believe what happened. If we had left just a minute earlier..."

No-one had anything to say in reply, and the room was filled with the sound of their heavy breathing. Standing in the doorway to the kitchen was a tired-looking man of around thirty years old. He glanced at his new night-time visitors in turn, and Abigail felt herself shrinking beneath his gaze. He kept glaring at her and frowning as if he didn't like what he was seeing.

"Are there any more of you?" he asked.

"No," replied Leo. "Not anymore."

The man gave a small nod. "What happened?"

Alenka gave a small snort, whilst Leo shrugged.

"They set him on fire," Abigail said in a small voice. She stared aimlessly at her feet as she spoke. "They set him on fire and he burned to death. I saw his face melting. Borys was my friend and the Germans killed him."

Alenka looked over at her. "He was my friend, too."

"Mine as well," agreed Leo.

"The Germans have killed the only friends I've ever had," Abigail added.

There was silence for a few moments.

"I'm Felek," announced the tired-looking man. "I don't have any friends left either."

Alenka looked up at him. "Just you here?"

Felek nodded. "There were three of us, but the other two went out several hours ago. They said they wanted to go and see the flags. I haven't seen them since."

Leo, Alenka, and Abigail all looked up at him in surprise. They had taken it for granted that everyone would have been able to see them no matter where they were in the ghetto.

"You may as well come upstairs," Felek yawned. "There's enough mattresses for all of us."

He leaned over and picked up the candle. Abigail seemed to have developed a new-found suspicion of fire, and she grimaced as the flame bounced and flickered around as if it were trying to leap out at them.

The four of them trooped upstairs and followed Felek into a room. It was larger than the one they had been cooped up in before which made things more bearable, although the window was like a block of blackness in the wall.

"This one's mine," Felek told them as he lay down on a mattress over in the corner. "I'll let you fight over the others."

Alenka chose the one nearest the window, leaving Abigail and Leo to share again. Both Alenka and Leo were asleep within a few minutes, but Abigail lay there wide awake for a while. Her brother's arm lay protectively across her as it usually did, and she knew he was asleep when it went limp.

Every time she closed her eyes, Abigail remembered how Borys had flailed and thrashed around as the flames ate away at his body. She tried to recall what his voice sounded like but the memory kept getting drowned out by his petrified screaming. Tears began to run down her face and she sobbed quietly to herself as everyone else around her slept. Her hand crept into the inside pocket that held the lock of hair she had taken from his head and as she twisted it between her fingers, it became easier to remember what he looked like and how he sounded. A smile appeared on her lips and the tears stopped soon afterwards. In her other pocket was the pistol, heavy and comforting against her side. Abigail hoped that there would be more Germans for her to shoot at tomorrow.

She gently kissed Leo's hand. "You're still my brave boy," she whispered.

\*\*\*

157

# Chapter 11

When Abigail woke up, she once again wondered where she was. Sunlight was streaming in through the window, making the room look far brighter and happier than it had been the night before. She spotted a black cat crawling across a roof and the smell of cooking was starting to waft in through the gap in the door.

A minute later the sound of footsteps was loud on the stairs. Just as they reached the top, Abigail closed her eyes again. She didn't want to be the only one who was awake when Felek came in. There was a loud noise as the door was shoved open and banged against the wall. Abigail felt Leo jerk awake next to her and she opened her eyes again.

"Breakfast, if anyone wants it," Felek announced.

A plate had been placed on the floor and it was stacked with sandwiches. Abigail spotted bits of meat poking out from between the bread, causing her stomach to rumble and they were all tucking in soon enough.

"Are you this generous to all your guests?" Alenka asked.

Felek shrugged. "We've been stockpiling food for a while. This is the last of the meat. If it tastes a bit off, that's probably because it is. It was either use it or throw it away."

Abigail *had* noticed that it tasted a bit tangy, but it was lovely to eat all the same. The dry bread wasn't a problem either.

"Any good?" Felek enquired.

Abigail and Alenka nodded dutifully, whilst Leo spoke for all of them.

"Yeah, iff nifth," he mumbled through a mouthful of bread.

"It's grilled," Felek told them. "No cooking oil for frying. Grilling is easier anyway. Don't ever boil beef."

Leo and Alenka exchanged a frown but didn't say anything.

"The bread is dry," observed Felek. "I would've soaked it in gravy or something, but we haven't got any."

"Nah, it's fine," Leo told him. "I can't even remember what fresh bread tastes like these days."

"I can. Mirek always managed to get fresh bread from somewhere. Piotr was the clever one who made sure our gas and water was always running."

"They the ones you mentioned last night?" Alenka asked.

"Yes," he answered. "What do those flags look like, by the way? It's what they went out for, to take a look at them. I told them that they're just bits of cloth yet they wouldn't listen."

"They're beautiful," Abigail blurted out.

Felek looked at her as if noticing her for the first time. "Really? I could've drawn some flags on the wall if they'd asked me. Mirek and Piotr aren't coming back."

Abigail shifted uncomfortably and found herself hoping that she was never left alone in the same room with Felek. He had a flat, monotone voice that was irritating to listen to and the things he said were peculiar. She wondered if Mirek and Piotr had simply run away because they found him so creepy.

"So, now that you're here, what's the plan?" asked Felek.

Alenka shrugged. "Sit tight and shoot any Germans who poke their heads up too far."

"Is that it? I'd hoped you were a rescue party."

Alenka rubbed her eyes. "Sorry to disappoint."

"Who's in charge?"

No-one said anything at first. "She's the oldest," Leo finally said, pointing at Alenka.

"I'm older than she is," Felek snapped.

Alenka suddenly felt ill. Whether it was because of the rotten meat or the inane questions she couldn't tell, but her patience was wearing thin.

"So what should we do, wise master?" she sarcastically asked.

"I don't know," he replied. "I thought you were here to rescue me."

Alenka put her head in her hands.

"What was your job before you were in the ghetto?" enquired Leo.

"I was a teacher."

Leo tried to hide a smile. "Did the kids set fire to your desk and smash your windows each week?"

Felek frowned. "No, I wouldn't tolerate anything like that. That's the problem with kids these days, no discipline. If only the parents would take more -"

159

Felek's eyes bulged as he saw what was in Abigail's hand. "Who gave you that? Why is a child carrying a gun around?"

"Don't kid yourself," Alenka told him. "She'd put a bullet in your eye from a mile away."

Felek's mouthed dropped open in disbelief.

"She'd even patch you up again afterwards," added Leo. "She's a cracking little nurse as well."

Abigail pulled a bandage out from her coat pocket. "It's my last one, so I don't want to waste it. Maybe you could paint some flags on it."

The three of them looked at each other and burst out laughing, leaving Felek to sit there with a dissatisfied frown on his face. He stood up and took the empty plate back downstairs.

Abigail leaned towards her brother. "I don't like him," she whispered.

Leo clapped her on the shoulder. "He's an odd one, but remember what I said before: if anyone upsets you, I'll shove my dirty socks in their face."

Abigail let out a giggle.

"Just point your pistol at him if he gets too overbearing," Alenka added. A sly smile appeared on her face. "Maybe kick him in the balls as well. He'll leave you alone after that."

Abigail laughed again. She had found Alenka intimidating at first, so it was nice to hear her being friendly and complimentary for once.

Felek clomped back up the stairs and sat back down on his mattress.

"The toilet is free by the way," he announced. "Just be sure to flush it afterwards and put the lid down."

Alenka turned her head and stared out the window.

"Good, I'll be back in a second," said Leo. He disappeared out the room and walked across the landing.

"Anything interesting going on outside?" enquired Felek.

"No, just bricks and misery as usual," replied Alenka.

"I could've told you that."

Alenka shot him an annoyed glance. "So, why didn't you?"

"Because you're nearest to the window, so I needed you to tell me."

Alenka and Abigail looked at each other. All of a sudden they were both glad that they were armed.

A heavy clanking, squealing sound cut through their thoughts. Although she knew what it was, Alenka stuck her head out the window anyway.

"Is that..." Abigail began.

"A tank," Felek finished.

The three of them looked at each other, their faces grave and worried. As the tank rolled closer, Abigail put her hands over her ears. Felek swallowed and turned pale, whilst Alenka took another look outside. She watched as it approached them and her heart lifted momentarily when she saw it stop - maybe it had broken down or was going to turn back around.

The tank's gun turret suddenly jerked upwards, and for an absurd moment Alenka was reminded of a moment from her childhood: she had been sharing a bath with her brother when they noticed that he had got an erection. Neither of them had ever seen one before and their loud laughter and splashing around caused their mother to come and see what all the fuss was about.

A wave of horror rushed through Alenka as she realised what was happening. Every hair on her body seemed to be standing on end, and out the corner of her eye she saw a figure standing in the doorway. She snapped her head round to shout a warning.

"Get out of -"

Leo stepped into the room and wondered what Alenka was screaming about. There was a sudden, blinding flash and the entire world seemed to slow down as a young girl floated right in front of him. She had long, dark hair and a pale face that was smooth and beautiful to look at. Her eyes were looking directly into his, kind eyes that knew nothing but love, and Leo felt himself being pulled into a special world that was full of warmth, a world that he had only been able to glimpse at before. A yellow circle of light surrounded the girl's head, shining brightly and radiantly through her hair. He reached out a hand to touch her but she vanished in an instant.

Leo's ears were consumed with a rushing, cracking sound that seemed to go on forever and it was like listening to the crackling of a fire being played back in slow motion. Dirt and debris swirled around him like leaves during autumn, whilst the air was hot and his chest felt heavy and useless.

Leo blinked and sat up, although he couldn't recall actually sitting down. For some reason he was covered in dust and the window was now much larger than it had been before. There was a squealing, clanking sound coming from somewhere and just in front of him was a large pile of broken concrete and bricks. Two legs were poking out, the feet clad in a smart pair of black shoes, shoes that would no doubt make an ideal birthday present for someone.

The realisation hit Leo like a sledgehammer and he lunged forwards.

"No! No, no, no!"

His hands grabbed wildly at the bricks and twisted lumps of wood piled up in front him.

"Abbie, hold on!" Leo screamed. "Just hold on!"

A hand pulled at his shoulder and a voice shouted in his ear. "Leo, she's gone!"

"No, I can see her, she'll be fine!"

"She's gone, we've got to go!" Alenka yelled, her voice cracking.

Leo shoved her away and began pulling at a large block of concrete. Alenka brought her rifle up and hit him with the butt.

"Leo, she's dead!" she screamed. "You can't save her! We've got to get out of here!"

Leo looked round at her, his face contorted with grief and fury. He blinked and saw that her face and lips were covered with dust, whilst his own hands were covered in cuts and blood. The entire room they had been staying in was nothing more than a wreckage and Felek was nowhere to be seen. Leo looked at his sister's legs again and saw how crushed and twisted they were: there was no way she could still be alive.

The clanking of the tank was getting louder and the stench of diesel exhaust fumes was almost choking. Alenka pulled Leo towards the stairs and this time he didn't try to fight her. Tears filled his eyes and it was all he could do to stop himself from tripping over his own feet. When they reached the ground floor a loud boom went off and the entire building shook, sending bricks and lumps of concrete flying down the stairs. In one of the adjoining rooms, a bike with a red frame and white-rimmed tyres fell over and clattered to the floor. For some reason the horizontal bar had a strip of cloth tied to it.

Leo and Alenka ran to the front door, both of them scrambling desperately to pull the handle down. They shoved the door open and Leo was vaguely aware of vehicles and men somewhere in the corners of his vision, but he ignored them and ran across the road. Whilst he was sure that the heavy footsteps behind him were Alenka's, he knew for certain that the shouts and the gunfire weren't. The pair of them ran between two buildings and kicked open the first door they came to.

Grief and exhaustion overwhelmed Leo and he slumped to the floor.

"They've taken everything I had! I've got nothing left!" he shouted, hot tears of rage running down his face.

Alenka bent down and threw her arms around him. "Leo, we can't give up now!" she yelled.

"Why not? What do we have?"

Alenka groped for an answer. She could feel the tendrils of defeat and despair taking hold of her. "We've got bullets, we've got a tunnel, we've got ourselves!"

"Bullets? They've got tanks and planes! And that tunnel may as well be on the other side of the world!"

Tears were welling up in Alenka's eyes. How had it all come to this? All that digging and planning, all the sneaking around... all the opportunities she had to go through the tunnel and never come back... what had it been for?

"Leo, I don't," she began. Her voice was cracking and there was a dry lump in her throat. "I don't know what..." although her mouth was moving, no words came out. She hugged Leo tighter and let the tears come on.

Leo shoved her away and screamed at the top of his lungs. He stood up and kicked at the wall, bellowing and cursing the Germans. Alenka shuffled away from him and hugged her knees in despair. There was a loud thud as the door flew open and banged against the wall. A soldier appeared in the doorway, his face twisted in an aggressive snarl. Leo fumbled for his pistol and pointed it at the soldier, who froze.

*Click*

*Click*
*Click*

Leo screamed and threw the useless weapon at the soldier. Alenka scrambled across the floor to pick up her rifle and managed to get a shot off. The German fell to the floor just as another one appeared behind him. The soldier fired his own gun and Alenka's entire body twisted around as something slammed against her shoulder. Another soldier darted forward and hit Leo across the head with a baton. Leo's knees buckled and he fell to the floor. The world around him started to go quiet and his vision began to fade away. The room seemed to be full of men in Nazi uniforms and three of them were kicking something in the corner. Leo turned his head to look and saw a blonde girl wearing a red cap. When he blinked and looked again he saw that she wasn't actually wearing anything on her head, but her hair was covered in blood. A tall man stood over Leo and seemed to throw something at him.

The world turned black.

***

# Chapter 12

Leo felt himself slowly waking up, unsure of how long he had been unconscious. Although his eyes were still closed, he somehow knew that he was in a safe place. He felt warm and content, almost as if his mother had just tucked him into bed like she did when he was a child. His ears were filled with silence but he didn't feel alone or vulnerable.

Leo lay there for a while longer and tried to open his eyes. At first nothing seemed to be working and he wondered if he was blind or paralysed. After what seemed like a lifetime, light began to slowly seep through his eyes. It was as if he was in a hospital and a doctor was gradually unwinding the bandages from his head. Soon, all he could see was a smooth whiteness all around him. Were they the white tiles of a medical ward?

*No, there are no nurses here. No-one needs nurses in this place.*

Or perhaps he was lying down in the garden, staring up at the clouds.

*No, there are no clouds here either  Storms and bad weather are not something you'll ever see.*

Was he looking at the smoke from a passing train? Sometimes he took Abigail to the nearby rail crossing so she could wave at all the passengers.

*You're closer to the truth than you probably realise.*

A face appeared above him, although it was blurred and he couldn't see who it was. Maybe it was a nurse.

*I've already told you, there are no nurses here.*

"Leo?" a soft voice enquired. It reminded him of how his mother would often tell him to mind the ants nests whenever he fell asleep in the garden.

*No ants will ever trouble you here.*

"Leo," the voice repeated. There was a tiny giggle that reminded him of how his sister would laugh when two trains passed by each other at once.

*Yes, there is plenty of joy and happiness here.*

"Leo!" the voice was louder and clearer this time, but there was no anger to it. It reminded him of that time when his sister had managed to get lost in the tall grass and had cried with relief when he found her again.

"Abbie?" it seemed to come out as a thought, rather than something he actually said out loud.

"Leo! You're safe now. I missed you."

Leo's vision began to clear and he found himself looking up into a pale, beautiful face. He wanted to reach out and touch it.

The girl giggled and flushed red. "Leo, you're so silly sometimes."

"What? Did you hear my...?"

"Don't worry, everything is confusing at first," Abigail reassured him. "Here, let me help you up."

Leo watched her bend down and in the blink of an eye he was standing up next to her. When he looked down at himself, he saw that he was barefoot. There also didn't seem to be any ground, just a sense of whiteness that he couldn't quite focus on. Abigail was wearing her birthday shoes and they looked brand new.

She smiled at him. "I never realised that it was you who chose them for me."

Leo returned the smile and reached out for her. When she embraced him, the knowledge that she was safe overwhelmed him. He closed his eyes and let the tears run down his cheeks. After some time she stepped away and slipped her hand into his.

"Come on, let me show you something," she said.

As they walked, Leo realised that he wasn't actually stepping on anything - it was like walking on incredibly soft sand. Off in the distance he saw two people sitting on a bench.

"Is that...?" he gasped.

"Yes. It's Mum and Dad. They've missed you as well, Leo. We all have."

Fresh tears appeared in Leo's eyes. He bent down and picked his little sister up, and she kissed him on the forehead.

"You're still my brave boy," she whispered.

\*\*\*


*Thank you for reading!*

*Independent authors such as myself rely heavily on reviews. Please consider leaving a rating of some kind from wherever you purchased this book.*

Email - mcargill79@gmail.com
Twitter - @MichaelCargill1
Facebook -
http://www.facebook.com/MichaelCargillAuthor
Website of hilarity - http://michaelcargill.wordpress.com

Made in the USA
Charleston, SC
06 January 2014